About the Author

Dean Backus is the author or co-author of over eleven plays, one of which ('Thus with a Kiss') was runner-up for Best Play at the 1993 Seattle New Playwrights Festival, and another ('Is This Seat Taken?') winning Best Play at the 1996 San Francisco Fringe Festival. He appeared in Alyson's 1998 anthology 'Wilma Loves Betty', and was featured in the book 'Gay Marriage Real Life' (2006) by Michelle Bates Deakin. His YA novel, 'Darts and Flowers', was published in 2022 by Torchflame Books. He lives outside of Portland, Oregan with his partner, Jonathan. Find him at www.deanbackusauthor.com.

THE DEEP END OF THE POOL

DEAN BACKUS

THE DEEP END OF THE POOL

Vanguard Press

VANGUARD PAPERBACK

© Copyright 2025
Dean Backus

The right of Dean Backus to be identified as author of
this work has been asserted by him in accordance with the
Copyright, Designs and Patents Act 1988.

A CIP catalogue record for this title is
available from the British Library.

ISBN 978-1-80016-809-1

*Vanguard Press is an imprint of
Pegasus Elliot Mackenzie Publishers Ltd.*
www.pegasuspublishers.com

First Published in 2025

**Vanguard Press
Sheraton House Castle Park
Cambridge England**

Printed & Bound in Great Britain

Dedication

To anyone who has walked through fire and come out the other side… This is dedicated to you.

Acknowledgements

Special thanks to Ron Austin, Lea Preciado, Julie Netherland, Christina Manetti, Brian Fey and Diane Williams — friends who helped me become a better person, along the way, and hopefully a better writer. Extra-special thanks to the sisters: Susanne, Emily and Sara.

Chapter 1

I am five years old in this memory, and attempting a flailing dog paddle from one end of the local community pool to the other. It's been one of those muggy, late-summer Seattle days, and now the water, though more than lukewarm, still feels better than the moist, heavy air. I try not to think about the hundreds of kids who were in and out of this pool today; more than a few of them probably peed in it.

My little string-bean arms and legs desperately churn in the darkening water. I do not look down at the bottom of the pool, where Monstro the whale, or various sea serpents may be waiting to rise, hungrily, towards my small, thrashing body. I do not look behind me, lest I realize how pathetic my progress has been and sink, exhausted, into the dark-aqua depths.

Instead, I keep my eyes on the distant glow of Frankie's cigarette; an orange cinder that lights up every time a drag is taken. In the dusky gloom, as the last lights fades in the sky, that little bit of orange is all that's keeping me afloat.

Above my splashing, I hear Frankie exhale a long disgruntled sigh and a cloud of smoke. The cloud envelops the salt-and-pepper hair that looks like it was chewed away instead of cut, the red-checkered flannel shirt, the worn jeans and work boots. Frankie's at least ten years older than my mother, and thus seems to me indescribably old, instead of probably just pushing forty, as I realized years later.

"Keep *going,* Shannon! Don't stop!"

The name *Shannon,* instead of my usual *Shan,* pierces my ear like a needle. I feel a burning in my lungs. My limbs feel like over-stretched rubber bands, and the chlorine is stinging my eyes, since I don't have goggles like the other kids. Frankie slipped the security guard a couple dollars to keep the pool open late for us, so I know better than to whine about goggles, or nose plugs, or flippers.

I complained — just once — about these late-evening swim sessions, and got a sharp cuff to the back of my head.

"What do you think I do this for? You think it's fun for me, after a long day at the warehouse, to drag an ungrateful, snot-nosed kid down to a pool and give up my hard-earned cash, so you can have some private practice time?"

The "hard-earned cash" actually came from my mother's Venice jar. She had a big, glass jar in the bedroom that she dropped her change and small bills into, and on the front of it she painted some canals and red and gold boats — gondolas, they call them — and these old-style buildings. She always said she was going to see Venice someday, but Frankie kept borrowing bills from it to pay for smokes, and bribing the guard so I could swim.

"Oh, Frankie," my mom sighed sadly, when she saw another wad of bills disappear from the jar.

"Do you want the kid to swim or not, Fiona? He's not even my kid, but I'm the one hauling his ass down to the pool three nights a week. So stop with the puppy-dog eyes." (My mother has big brown eyes, like I do, and when she's sad she really does look like a kicked puppy.)

Thinking about my mom makes me kick harder and faster. I slice through the water like a baby shark, letting the rage and anger propel me. I keep my eyes forward, staring at the white concrete wall with the blue-tile trim around the edge, as it zooms towards me, faster and faster. But now I'm out of control. I can't slow down; I'm coming in too fast. There's a THUNK sound as my head hits the wall, then the thick, salty, sickening taste of blood gushing from my nose.

Frankie stabs out the cigarette in disgust. "Oh, Jesus, Shan — what'd you do that for? They're not going to let us keep coming back here if you bleed all over the pool. Don't you have a brain in your head? God *damn.*"

I am yanked out of the pool by one arm, and swaddled roughly into my threadbare towel — one of the older bath ones which has been demoted to Swim Duty. A grimy handkerchief is thrust under my nostrils, and a drill sergeant's bark: "Keep it there!" Frankie hustles me out of the gate before the wheezing, sweaty guard returns from his regular trip to the snack machine. He is fat and surly and always gets two bags of chips and a soda — sometimes even an ice-cream sandwich — but he has never offered me even one, single chip.

We drive towards home, the darkness and the heat once again enveloping me. I lean against the hard metal of the truck door, wrapped in my fraying towel, trying to keep my head back, hoping the blood running down my throat doesn't make me puke. Streetlights turn on, showing swarms of black insects — mosquitos or gnats, maybe — frantically dancing in circles under the sickly, yellow glow. An old, country guy on the radio is singing about wanting to melt "your cold, cold heart." I think about orange popsicles, and my stomach lurches.

I don't talk to Frankie, and Frankie doesn't talk to me. We drive the ten minutes' home in silence, listening to the sad, country man, not looking backwards or sideways, but just staring straight ahead.

That way, you can hopefully always see what's coming at you.

Chapter 2

"Just keep swimming, just keep swimming…"

You wouldn't think a sixteen-year-old guy with a swimming scholarship to a new, private school, a couple of local records notched in his belt, and some decent good looks (my mom says I'm starting to look like Anthony Perkins, the old movie star) would have a mental tape loop constantly playing Dory, the spacey blue tang fish, voiced by Ellen DeGeneres in *Finding Nemo*, would you?

Appearances can be deceiving.

"You're Shan Milne, aren't you?"

I turned towards the voice and closed my locker, giving the combination a spin. As I did, I worked really hard not to let my jaw go slack and my mouth drop open, also like some sort of fish.

The girl who had just spoken to me looked like something out of Celtic mythology. She had this raven-black hair, pale skin, and the most amazing eyes I'd ever seen. They were this deep, dark green; the color you seen in mountain pools when you're hiking in the Cascades. I've jumped into a couple of those pools on hot days, and they're always a lot deeper — and *much colder* — than you'd think.

I suddenly realized that even though she'd seemed to ask me a question, she didn't really. Her tone of voice was matter-of-fact, like she was just seeking confirmation of something she already knew. Also, she used the abbreviated *Shan* instead of *Shannon.* My throat suddenly went dry, so my reply came out sort of raspy: "Yeah. Who wants to know?"

She smiled delightedly, and hugged her books to her chest like they were armor. She was wearing a deep blue sweater, a plaid skirt, and what looked like riding boots, so she was almost my height. As she took a step towards me, I smelled some sort of exotic, vanilla perfume. "I'm Kallie Corcoran. My mom is one of the parent volunteers here, and she was helping stuff the Welcome Packets for the new students." She smiled again, pulling the books even tighter (was she *trying* to show off the stretching sweater?), I noticed. "She told me to look out for you."

"Me?" I was flattered, but nervous. Throughout most of elementary and junior high school, most kids didn't seem to notice me much, and the few that did were usually looking for reasons to shove me into lockers, or occasionally deposit me in garbage cans. Then I had my "growth spurt" (if you call becoming a human beanstalk a "spurt") and started winning at swim meets, and I got somewhat more popular, even if I didn't feel comfortable making close friends with many people. It was after I set a district record that The Jefferson Academy (not *Jefferson* Academy; *The* Jefferson Academy) sent my mom a letter, basically saying I could come here on a scholarship for eleventh and twelfth grade, as long as I was on the swim team.

This girl — Kallie — kept smiling and looking at me like I was some sort of chess board, and she was deciding how she wanted to set up her pieces. "Yeah. I did some research on you after my mom told me about you. So, you're like the new school swimming star."

I felt a warm blush rush over me, and my face got hot. Without thinking, I scratched the back of my neck, another nervous tic I have when I'm flustered or nervous. "Yeah, well… I did okay last year."

"*Okay?* I saw some footage of you on the Web. You were like, *amazing.*" I didn't think she could step much closer, but she did; her breath smelled like strawberry Bubblicious. "And my mom and the pictures on the Web did *not* do you justice. You are… scrum-diddly," she breathed, quoting *Charlie and the Chocolate Factory*, one of my favorite books.

If I wasn't already intrigued before, I sure was now. I'd never interacted with a girl — with anyone — like this in my life. "Well, uh… thanks," I croaked, probably dazzling her with my rapier-sharp wit. "Maybe I'll see you later in one of my classes? I'm still figuring out my schedule."

"Not if I see you first," she purred. She really did: she sounded like a giant kitty cat who'd just been given the world's most delicious mouse. Giving me one last dazzling smile with her curvy lips, and the world's fastest wink from one emerald eye, she turned and eased her way down the hall.

I stood there, momentarily rooted in place like some sort of tree. A girl talked to me — no, a girl flirted with me. A *hot* girl flirted with me. Kids at my previous school had been nice to me, especially in the last year and a half, but it always felt somehow distant and a little grudging: "Oh, now we know he can win stuff, so I guess we'll be nicer to him." The fact that I wasn't always able to have friends home, due to my mom's work schedule and the couple years we spent moving around post-Frankie, didn't help.

But this girl, Kallie, sought *me* out. She *wanted* to know me, and it was a pretty big head rush, let me tell you. If I wasn't already close to six feet tall, I would've sworn I'd just shot up another half a foot over the past five minutes.

Five minutes? Jeez. I consulted my schedule: I was late for Physics, and I was still trying to figure out the layout of *The* Jefferson Academy. Coming from a comparatively modern glass-and-cement public school to a brick-and-ivy relic from the twentieth century was confusing, especially the way the original, dark, little hallways bumped up against newer additions and extensions, past and present violently colliding in strange and unexpected ways.

I pulled the already-worn school map from my pocket and studied it. Fortunately, my Science room was right around the corner. If I hauled ass, I could make it before the second bell. I started trucking.

My first day of eleventh grade, two periods in, and I already had a hot girl trying to chat me up. This day could not possibly get any better!

Chapter 3

In Science, it got a whole lot worse. Well, not worse; let's just say *surreal*.

I was sitting at one of the long lab tables in the back, minding my own business, letting the dandruffy teacher do his opening monologue about the wonders of force, motion, attraction, etc., and trying not to look at the numerous jars up in the cabinets, which seemed to be filled with various preserved animals in states of suspended animation. Then, abruptly, this kid in front of me turned around and whispered, "Hey."

"Hey," I said, a little coolly; a defense mechanism from the old days when people came on a little too strongly, or asked too many questions. This kid had — there's no other polite way to say this — a body which was definitely *not* an athlete's. He was majorly stocky to the point of being fat, and seemed awash in an oversized Yankees' baseball jersey, along with the accompanying backwards-turned hat. I had a sudden flashback to Frankie watching a Yankees game, and me standing in front of the TV while eating a handful of peanuts. I was still blocking the view of the TV when New York hit a home run, and was rewarded with a slap so hard, I saw stars for an hour. To this day, I can't stand the smell of peanuts, so my mom tells everyone I have an allergy.

Anyways, this kid had big old sausage legs stuffed into jam-style shorts, and a big, gooney smile on his wide, pink face — not a flirtatious smile, like Kallie had; more like one of those guileless little-kid smiles. He stage-whispered to me, "You don't have a lab group yet, do you?"

"No," I muttered back, trying not to make eye contact, which unfortunately meant staring at what looked like a jarred pig fetus. "It's my first day here, and I didn't know we needed one."

"Oh, you *do*," he said, rather theatrically. The teacher at the front of the room paused, shot us the hairy eyeball, then resumed droning on. The kid lowered his voice. "You've got to have the right lab partners in Science classes, or your labs go straight to hell. As the new kid, you probably didn't know that."

He smiled and looked at me expectantly, like he was waiting for me to thank him for this brilliant insight and his compassion for me, the assumed Poor Fatherless Waif All Alone In The World.

I put on my best tough-guy voice, the one — thanks to Sam Elliott — that had saved me from the trash can once or twice. "So, you're the supposed genius who's going to show me how things work around here?"

The kid didn't get the sarcasm; it seemed to fly right over his head, like a Frisbee. "*We* are going to adopt you. Me and Sonya," he said, pointing to my left.

I now realized that most of this little conversation had been observed by a quietly smiling African-American girl, with a soft, curly mane of hair and a red-chili-pepper blouse. Her skin, unlike the first kid's pink flush, was the color of chai. She was as gorgeous as Kallie had been, but in a completely different way.

"We're the outcasts around here," she said sweetly.

"Clean cup, clean cup, move *down!*" Happy Mouth caroled, grabbing his and Sonya's books and moving into the unoccupied chair to my right as she slid around and flanked me on the left. I was suddenly as stuck as peanut butter between two slices of bread. "Welcome to the Mad Tea Party! I'm the Mad Hatter: a.k.a. Zip."

"Zip?" I was momentarily so thrown by his forwardness that I couldn't process all of the data flooding my mental inbox.

"It was short for Zipporah," Sonya murmured, glancing knowingly past me with a penetrating gaze. She seemed to have his number.

"Sonya!" Zip looked genuinely shocked and hurt for a moment. His face crumbled. "You're not supposed to—"

"Oh, I know, I *know,*" Sonya said, her voice rising to convey a certain weariness. "Just dial it *down* for a few, you're going to scare this poor boy. Now — as you heard, at *ear-splitting* decibels, I'm Sonya, and this is Zip." She raised her eyebrows pointedly. "And you are?"

"Shan," I mumbled, my eyes on the teacher still going over the class syllabus amidst a hubbub of side conversations from the class. For once, I actually wanted to be called out by a teacher, if only to end this increasingly weird conversation.

"Shan?" Zip looked confused.

I tried not to sigh in frustration as I explained this for the ten thousandth time in my life: "It's short for Shannon. It's Irish."

"What's your middle name?" Sonya asked, nodding matter-of-factly. I wondered if, as a Black girl, she occasionally had well-meaning but clueless people ask her if she was part Russian.

"Peter. Shannon Peter Milne."

"He's like Pe-tah Pan!" Zip breathed, so enchanted that he developed a spontaneous British accent. "He's going to fly us to Neverland, so we don't have to grow up!"

"No danger there," Sonya countered, rolling her eyes towards me. However I felt about Zip, I was beginning to like Sonya. She continued, pointedly, to Zip, "And honey, you, of *all* people, should know better than to tease people about their name."

"What kind of a name is Zipporah?" I asked, trying to be polite. It sounded seriously old-fashioned and definitely didn't seem to match its owner.

"Hebrew," Zip said, suddenly somewhat terse. I wondered if this was a sore spot, then I realized that the teacher was actually calling roll, and was a couple names in. "Chaikin, Zipporah?"

"Zip, please," Zip said, turning to face the front of the room, profile suddenly stiff and on alert.

"It says Zipporah," the teacher said, looking confusedly at his roster.

"I go by Zip." A flush of color went up Zip's face, changing it from pleasant pink to deep red. I wondered about it for a split second, then felt a wave of empathy for him; in a few names, I was going to have to offer my own correction, followed by the usual titters and giggles.

The teacher had returned to his roster. "Hawkins, Rose; Jipat, Evan; Kistle, Jeff; Larkin, Sonya—"

"Present, Mr Farthing," Sonya said, waving her arm and speaking in a strong, clear voice I wasn't expecting. Then she did something even more surprising: she laid her hand on my arm and said, "And this is Shan Milne. He likes to be called Shan."

"Shan," Mr Farthing said, pronouncing it as though it were a rare chemical compound. He made a note on his sheet. "I'm not at 'M' yet, but thank you, Sonya. Lew, Chay?"

I was so stunned for a moment, I couldn't think straight. Sonya pulled her hand from my arm and smiled knowingly at me; I couldn't help but grin back. At the same time, I felt a gentle nudge against my right arm, and Zip whispered, "We're definitely riding the same wave, bud."

I wasn't sure about that, yet, but it did seem that this pond I was going to be swimming in suddenly got a lot warmer and cozier.

Chapter 4

The rest of the day wasn't bad, as far as first days go. You know it's a good sign when only one teacher actually gives out homework: reading and journaling for a page on a Rudyard Kipling poem for English, "A Ripple Song." All of my other teachers just had us pick up textbooks and went over the syllabus.

Sonya was in my English class, and made a point to sit next to me again. She didn't say much, just occasionally made eye contact with me when the teacher — one of those young, bearded, sport coat and elbow patches types — said something funny, and her lips would curl into a slow half-smile. I would've found it kind of hot, to tell the truth, except Kallie was also in this class.

She showed up just as the bell rang, when almost all the seats were occupied, and after she scanned the room and saw that there was nothing next to me, she offered a mock-pout of her sexy lips, then smiled and took a seat in the back corner. Sonya didn't say anything, but when I turned back from Kallie I noticed she'd been watching our little pantomime with an expression of polite curiosity. I wondered if they knew each other, but after class everyone bolted for the door while the teacher, Mr Graves, asked me what I'd been reading at my last school. (American classics: *Huckleberry Finn*, *Moby Dick*, *Ethan Frome*, *The Grapes of Wrath*.) I couldn't tell if he was genuinely interested, or doing that let's-see-if-the-dumb-jock-actually-knows-anything probe some teachers do. When I got out of there, both Sonya and Kallie had already disappeared.

Before lunch I had gym, and Zip was in my class. He changed in a bathroom stall, I assume because he was embarrassed about his weight. All we did was a basic fitness test, consisting of running four laps around the gym, then doing various stretches and exercises while we hopped/danced/skipped back and forth across the cavernous space. The last part of the class was "free ball," and the white and handful of Black kids played four-on-four basketball, while a few Latino kids on the sidelines tried to form a breakaway soccer game. Based on my height, I got tapped for basketball, which was pretty darn funny considering that Zip was right next to me for most of the game, even though he was barely five feet five, giving me a blow-by-blow of everyone in the gym: who was a stoner; who used to be a stoner but was now clean; who was dating whom; who used to be dating whom; who hoped to be dating whom in the future, etc. etc. It was better than a real-time Facebook feed. He ran around the court, mostly just getting in the way of the other team, but that was great for us: we won the game, sixteen to ten, in thirty minutes.

After the game I took a quick shower, just to get the sweat off, but I knew I'd be swimming after school and would thus have to take shower number three for the day then, so I made it fast. Zip again gathered his gym bag and trundled off to the bathroom stall; when he came back from changing clothes, he sat on the edge of the bench facing the door, waiting for us all to be released. It was the only time — except for the bit in Science, with his name — when he seemed out of his element and uncomfortable. He kept his eyes on the floor and just waited for the bell to ring, oblivious to the slamming of lockers and the hooting, hollering and barrage of cuss words filling the air from some twenty jacked-up, overly-hormonal guys. I don't always feel comfortable with the way guys talk in the locker room, but what can you do? Guys will be guys.

At lunch, Zip personally escorted me through the lunch line (sandwiches, yes; anything fried, yes; anything with sauce, no) to Sonya's table. We all agreed that the day was going pretty well — at least, no kid had opened fire with a shotgun yet, which seems to be some sort of scary benchmark these days.

I was just dumping my tray and getting ready to leave the commons area, when Kallie suddenly stepped in front of me.

"Where were you?" she asked, in a borderline accusatory tone.

I was thrown by the edge in her voice and the sudden storm clouds appearing in those green eyes. I swallowed and my heart jumped at bit, the way it does during confrontations. "I didn't see you. I was sitting with my friends."

"I was right *there*," Kallie said, pointing behind us to a table in the corner of the cafeteria, where several other girls in similar outfits were giving me frosty looks. "Didn't you want to sit with me? You didn't hold a place for me in English, either."

"I didn't know we were in the same class," I said, stammering a little bit. Off to the side, I was vaguely aware of Sonya and Zip watching this drama unfold, Zip looking worried and Sonya looking coolly annoyed. "And Zip brought me through the lunch line. I just… didn't see you."

"Well, you didn't look very hard," Kallie sniffed, her mouth a hard line. The warm, playful girl from this morning seemed to have disappeared. She'd been replaced with someone whose words sounded like they were chipped out of ice. "So, can I come watch you at swim practice after school, if that's not a problem? I mean, if it is, I don't *have* to — if your other *friends* are going to be there." She said the word *friends* as if she was referring to something dusty and sticky she'd found under the refrigerator.

"We have plans," Zip said, unexpectedly. "Sonya and I are planning on doing homework and catching up on some *Game of Thrones*. So no, we won't be there."

"We'd *assumed*," Sonya intoned in a voice that sounded like a Samurai sword being unsheathed, "that

Shan wouldn't want a lot of pressure on his first day swimming here. You know, considering he's the one who's actually the swimming star… not us." She shot Kallie a look of lethal contempt, as if she were a blue-sweatered cockroach. "Shan, you don't mind that we're not there?"

"Sure," I said, completely lost by now at all the dynamics whizzing around me. "I mean, yeah, for a first day… it's okay if you have other plans. But if Kallie wants to come and watch…" I was fumbling all over the place, trying to please everyone. Three pairs of eyes stared at me, and I felt my face begin to flush. "I mean, I'm okay with it. If the coaches don't mind."

"Coach Corcoran," Kallie said, smiling with some of the early-morning dazzle she'd first shown me, "is my uncle. I don't think he'll mind me sitting in as a spectator." She flicked her eyes at Sonya, in a *check-mate* move. "So, I'll see you at the pool around three thirty!"

As she said this, she brushed by me like a cat does in that way that mixes affection with showing you who's really the boss. She leaned in and just barely brushed her lips against my ear, letting a little bit of her breath tickle the inner hairs, and my whole body got the shivers. I had to adjust my posture for a moment, so as not to give anything away if anyone was staring at my nether regions.

Sonya was watching Kallie return to her friends; her face was flooded with distaste. But Zip was looking at me with a mixture of apology and fearfulness. "Sorry, Shan. I didn't know…"

"It's okay," I said, clapping his beefy shoulder lightly. Here I'd just made two new friends this morning, as well as met a hot girl, and now the whole dynamic had shifted when Kallie had come over. "I just met her this morning; it's not like we're dating or anything."

"Not yet," Sonya said, her voice as flat and dry as the New Mexico desert.

"What's that mean?" I asked, a little defensively.

"Let me tell you something about Kallie Corcoran," Sonya said, very deliberately linking her arm through mine as she guided Zip and me out of the commons area. "She's not a girl who's used to hearing the word *No*. So if you're even *thinking* about dating her, you'd better start figuring how high you're gonna go when she says 'Jump.'"

"Shan's a big boy," Zip said, a little defensively, as if he was somehow protecting me from Sonya — or both girls. This irritated me for some reason. "He can do what he wants. It's only his first day here, remember? There's lots of fish in the sea."

"Oh, you did not *even* refer to girls as 'fish,'" Sonya shot back, giving Zip a little shove.

"It's a Motown song!" Zip protested, now laughing. "Seriously, I'll play it on my phone for you later! Don't hurt me!"

They chased each other down the hall, on their way to another class, Zip still shrieking, *"Don't hurt me!"* as Sonya swung at him, and both of them laughing and laughing.

As I stood in the hallway, oceans of kids passing around me on all sides like schools of minnows, I thought of a quote I read once from Woody Allen, where he said "Comedy is tragedy, plus time."

But I wondered, sometimes, how long some things needed to be left in the past before they were funny.

Chapter 5

On land, I often feel gangly and uncoordinated, as if none of my limbs are working in conjunction with each other. I also worry about saying the wrong thing, and upsetting people, and in general being in the way.

In the water, none of this matters; everything coheres, and my body becomes a lean, slicing machine, cruising from one end of the pool to the other, hardly thinking about it.

I was hauled out of the water by Coach Corcoran, who turned out to be a tanned, good-looking middle-aged Irish guy who looked like he should sell insurance. Right next to him was Coach Tsai, an Asian bulldog of a man in his early thirties. They were staring at their stopwatches like they'd just witnessed the Second Coming.

"One-oh-five!" Coach Tsai exclaimed, almost screaming with happiness. "*One-oh-five* on a hundred-meter freestyle! Have you been training this summer?"

"Not really," I said, fudging the truth a bit. One of my mom's regular customers, who'd known me for about four years, was a retired widower, and had a pool he hardly ever used, sticking mostly to the hot tub for his arthritis. So during the summer, I biked over to his house three or four mornings a week for an hour or so, but it was hardly serious conditioning. If I'd been training regularly, I'd probably be on the road to Michael Phelps-dom.

"Well, you're a firework for sure," Coach Corcoran said, smiling like a guy who's just found something that's going to put his name into a state record book. "Looks like my niece is pretty impressed with you, too."

No one could miss her. Kallie had hand-lettered a giant sign reading "GO SHAN!" and was waving it from the bleachers. Any storm clouds from lunch had been definitively chased away: she was back to glowing with excitement, and her dark hair was bouncing all over the place, along with the rest of her. It was hard — er, *difficult* — to look at her for very long.

The rest of the guys on the team seemed happy for me, too, which was nice; usually, there's at least one hotshot who's decided that you're obstacle number one to his becoming a school or state champion, and has it out for you. But these guys were all clapping and smiling and whistling, as if I were already accepted as one of them. I felt a warm feeling flood my chest, as if permafrost I'd never even realized I'd built up inside over the years was finally cracking and thawing.

"That was *really* good, dude," this one blond-haired kid — Theo — said, putting his hand up for me to shake and pulling me into a quasi-hug. I felt a little weird hugging another guy while wearing a Speedo — especially a guy I'd just met, who looked like a hunky version of Tom Sawyer — but he seemed fine with it, so I relaxed and enjoyed the sensation of being hugged. Aside from my mom, I don't get hugged very often. Or ever.

At the end of practice, we were all heading towards the locker room, towels around the shoulders and me still collecting pats on the shoulder and good vibes, and then out of nowhere Kallie was bouncing in front of me. "You did great!"

"Thanks," I said, unconsciously looking around to see who might be watching us. Was I glad to be seen with her, or did I suddenly have a weird feeling like I was cheating on Sonya and Zip?

"I made you a sign," Kallie said, obviously. "I wasn't sure if you saw it or not. I thought it might give you some encouragement and help calm your nerves."

I saw it, all right; the whole team saw it. Presumably, people in space saw it. But I didn't want to diss her for doing something nice. "That's awesome, thanks."

"You're welcome." The sparkle was definitely back in her eyes. She adjusted the poster under her arm so it blocked the view from the coaches, who were still standing on the far side of the pool, talking. Without taking her eyes off of me, she ran her hand very deliberately down my stomach… and right on down across the front of my swimsuit. An expected reaction promptly occurred.

"Kallie, what are you doing?" I almost hissed, jumping. I didn't want to smack her hand away, but the little hop at least gave us a bit of space between us. Briefly.

"What?" she said, smiling guilelessly, reaching again. My body did that weird convulsion thing guys do, when trying to avoid getting hit in the nuts, or other activities. I doubled over and lifted one leg, trying to block her hand. Unfortunately, she seemed to take this as encouragement in the game.

"Don't!" I said, trying not to yelp and attract attention from any other random spectators still hanging around. My moments of glory and adulation of a few moments ago were gone; now I felt a rush of embarrassment, and somehow dirty, like a little boy being caught doing something bad, even though I wasn't the one who was doing anything wrong.

"So, I think you should come over for dinner tomorrow night," Kallie said, not missing a beat. "You should meet the rest of my family. And I'll ask my uncle to come, too." She reached for my crotch again, a devilish smile curling from her lips. "Say yes?"

"Kallie—"

"And not you and your mom, just you. Say *yes*," she said, grabbing for my penis. I turned a bit to deflect, and she (accidentally?) hit me right in the nuts. I let out a groan of pain.

"Is that a yes?" She was all over me now, grabbing at me, tickling me. I'd never had this happen to me before in my life, and I was completely flustered. There's no way people weren't watching this.

I finally realized I was still wearing my towel around my neck, and seized it, wrapping it around my waist, pushing her hands away. "Okay, okay! Yes! YES!"

"Are you sure?" She was slightly out of breath, and her face was contorted with a smile of almost crazed glee, as if this whole thing had been a turn-on for her. She looked a little frightening, but also blazingly alive. I pulled the towel tighter around my mid-section.

"Yes, I'm sure. I'll be there. We can leave right after practice. Is it okay if I bike?"

"Bike?" She acted as though I'd spoken a foreign language. "Leave your bike here. I have a BMW convertible. I'll drive, and I'll bring you back here after dinner to pick it up."

"Okay."

"Okay!" she said, very brightly, all sweetness and light again. And this time she really did kiss me, right on my neck, and I felt a slight scrape of her teeth against my jaw. She did a tiny wave, then walked away.

I stood there for a moment, still with my towel wrapped around me, but feeling totally exposed. *What the hell just happened?*

I turned, feeling somewhat numb, and headed for the locker room. I passed Theo on the way in, still in his swimsuit with his towel over his shoulder, looking at me as a jumble of emotions played across his face, but he didn't say anything. Just as well. At that moment, I probably couldn't have had of any sort of coherent conversation.

Chapter 6

The sun was just beginning to set by the time I biked into the parking lot of the Excelsior Inn, and the sun looked like a scoop of melting sherbet behind the old building. I locked my bike and wandered through the lobby, heading into the restaurant to the left, but not before glancing automatically in the coffee shop to the right.

I should explain. The Excelsior is a classic old hotel from way back in the 1920s or 30s, and at one time there was a little restaurant just off the lobby. When they did a remodel some fifty years later, they turned the old restaurant into a coffee shop with a handful of little booths, an L-shaped counter with stools, and a small grilling area where the cook makes simple breakfasts (the Hawaiian omelet with ham, cheese, and pineapple is out of this world), and grilled sandwiches for lunch. The coffee shop closes at three in the morning.

Across the lobby, after they were done renovating a chunk of the old lobby area and part of an adjacent patio, they put in a nicer seafood-themed restaurant with white table cloths, deep blue walls, a huge fish tank behind the host stand… the works. It's always bright and fluorescent in the coffee shop, as the walls are deep yellow with red booths and trim; the seafood restaurant, called "Catch", is much darker and more elegant. As far as I can tell, "elegant" means a bowl of clam chowder and a half sandwich in the coffee shop will run you five dollars; over at Catch, it's seven ninety-nine. I personally wouldn't pay three dollars just for so-called "elegance," but it doesn't matter, since I don't pay for it anyways. My mom pays for me, and the cost is half the menu price — the coffee-shop menu price. Two-fifty for dinner isn't a bad deal, and the food is really good.

My mom sometimes works as the morning coffee-shop server, and since there's usually only two servers in there, she does gangster tips if she works an eight-hour shift. Sometimes, however, they have her work half a shift in the coffee shop, then have her come over and work at Catch for the early evening shift — sometimes as a server, sometimes as a hostess. She keeps a long black skirt and a nice blouse in her locker in case she needs to change from one job to the other; presto, off with the coffee shop uniform or the embroidered Catch shirt (the letters are all different nautical animals and themes embroidered into a logo), and into the "fancy-schmancies" as she calls them. It can be a long day sometimes, especially if they give her an hour off between shifts to hang out or run errands, but on a good day she can walk out with a couple hundred dollars, including tips. Claud, the General Manager, is really good about always making sure she puts down for time and a half if he keeps her even fifteen minutes past eight hours, which he does at least three or four times a week. Then he gives her two free meals, too, one of which she often uses for me.

Tonight she was hostessing, wearing the long, black skirt, a cream-colored blouse and the only necklace my dad ever gave her before he left: it's gold, with her birthstone, an emerald, set in a heart. Her hair was down and she'd put on extra makeup. She looked kind of like the actress Demi Moore, only a little more careworn if you looked deep in her eyes.

When she saw me, though, they brightened up. "Shan!" she said, pulling me close and giving me a quick kiss on the cheek, even though I'm really too old for this sort of thing by now. She was busy stuffing the menus with updated specials for the night, while the wait staff darted about behind, lighting candles, like oversized lightning bugs. "How was your day, honey?"

I half-hugged her, feeling a momentary pang as I realized she was getting smaller than me — or was I growing taller? Either way, things were definitely changing between us. "Good. I did one-oh-five in my swimming tryout."

"Is that good?" After almost a decade of me in and out of various pools, my mom still couldn't keep up with what was a 'good' or 'bad' time in the swimming world.

"Pretty good." Actually, very good. "I could do better."

"You will." She smiled at me, and I felt another pang in my heart. She deserved so much better. "Did you meet anyone nice?"

I leaned back against the wall, watching the neon tetras in the tank behind her dart about as she grabbed menus, stuffed them into the holders, and set them aside. "A couple cool kids. Oh, and this… girl wants me to have dinner at her house tomorrow."

"A *girl?*" My mom's eyebrows lifted and she smiled wickedly, the fish tank casting cool colors and reflections off of her face. "Since when do you have dinner with *girls*? And after your first day, no less?"

This was why I don't like to discuss personal stuff with my mother. I figured a tiny fudge of the truth, or just withholding a few key details, wouldn't hurt. "Her uncle is my swim coach. She saw me swim, and asked me over. Thought it couldn't hurt." All more or less true.

My mom slid the last menu into its place and briskly gathered them into a pile, neatly dropping several of them into the slot next to the stand. The glowing computer screen on the desk, I noticed, indicated near-continuous reservations from five thirty on, which meant that this conversation couldn't go on for much longer. Still, she touched my face again, and gave me the puppy-dog eyes. "I'm so proud of you, Shan. And bonding with your coach is a great thing for you. Those are the sorts of people who can write you recommendation letters for college, introduce you to important people. Make sure you wear a tie."

"I don't have a clean tie," I lied. I hated wearing ties: they made me feel constrained, like I might choke and asphyxiate myself at any moment.

"Your blue and purple one with the fleur-de-lis is clean. I just picked it up from the cleaners a week ago." Damn, she was too smooth sometimes. Still, I was grateful she was focused on the coach. I was afraid Mom was going to have me and Kallie married off before I even introduced them. Focusing on the coach was a good thing.

I must've had some sort of relieved expression cross my face as I was thinking about what I wasn't telling her, because she smiled and said, "See? When you're ready for great things, great things come to you. Oh honey…" Her eyes actually started to tear up a bit as she grabbed my hand, and her voice dropped to a near-whisper. "Things are going to change for us. For you. I can feel it now. Networking is going to be huge for you. Always make sure you're putting your best foot forward."

"Yeah," I drawled. "I'll make sure not to fart too much at dinner, or blow my nose on the drapes."

"*Stop!*" my mother said, giving me a little shove and gesturing for me to follow her. She knows I always like to sit in the back booth, closest to the kitchen, where there's an occasional belch of steam or the hiss of something delicious hitting the grill, and sometimes the burst of Spanish from the workers followed by hearty, sandpapery laughter. I slid into the booth as she offered me the menu, and just shook my head. "The usual."

"Half BLT and a bowl of chowder?" I nodded. "I'll tell Sheila to ring it in."

Sheila is my favorite waitress; a big-hipped redhead with denim-blue eyes who's never forgotten or gotten an order wrong in some twenty-plus years of working at the Excelsior. Even though I don't pay for dinner, I always leave her a buck and some change as a thank you. Since my mom gives me my allowance, I guess it's all Circle of Life anyways.

I settled into the booth, looking at the candles sparkling on each table, each one waiting for someone to sit down with them, like little homing beacons. Little symbols of warmth and comfort and temporary security, for as long as dinner lasted. It was a Monday, so the chances of a wedding proposal tonight weren't real likely. I always liked it when that happened, even if more than half the time you could tell the bride-to-be wasn't really fooled or surprised when it happened. But they pretended, all the same.

I watched an elderly couple come in, my mom gliding across the floor as she took them to their window table while the other servers finished their prep work or sampled tonight's specials (rockfish, bacon-wrapped asparagus, rose-flavored crème brulée). I envied the old married people for just a moment, imagining their lives. Everything was behind them now: all the worry, all the uncertainty, all the "what am I going to *do* with my life?" All they had to do was play with their grandkids, hopefully not get too sick for too long, and eventually die at home in their sleep. Peace, at last.

The old guy held the chair out for the lady, her hair a gray cloud, a green and brown scarf swaddled around her shoulders. She sank into it gratefully. He wore a dark sport coat with little flecks of color in it. Not tourists; they probably came here for some special occasion. It was unlikely they'd stay overnight; they'd miss the feather beds in the hotel rooms, the starched linens, the coffee service with vintage silver pots lining the lobby in the mornings, the old-style tiling in the bathrooms. My mom and me had lived here "off the books" for a couple months once, when I was younger, and I'd gotten way too comfortable and used to it. Now I knew better than to settle in and get too relaxed.

My phone buzzed, and I jolted. I'd forgotten it was on. I almost never use it, but my mom had given me one last year "for emergencies." The only thing was, I was here, and Mom was right around the corner in the restaurant. Who would be texting me?

I swiped the screen and clicked the "message" icon: up it popped.

CAN'T WAIT FOR TOMORROW. SO EXCITED. MOM DAD AND UNCLE R 2. SEE YOU L8ER. XXOO K.

I stared at the screen, bewildered, as Sheila placed the plate of food next to me. I didn't even look at it; my stomach was doing the sort of flips it usually saves for when I'm standing atop a high-diving board, looking down at the water far below.

I hadn't given Kallie my number.

Chapter 7

The next morning was a stress-out. Not only did I have to worry about my swim gear, along with my regular clothes, I had to also think about what I was going to wear to Kallie's that night. Wearing a tie and dress shirt all day would've called attention to myself, so I was stuck between two dilemmas, either of which would make me a sweaty mess but for different reasons: asking my mom to drive me to school, which would've meant more questions and pep-talk, or cramming everything into my backpack along with balancing an additional bag on the back of my bike for the two-mile ride to school. (Fortunately, I'd only had to bring one book home yesterday for homework.)

It was a snap decision.

"Nice bike," Sonya said as I was locking up in front of the school. She looked as if she'd been waiting for me, and was rocking a deep green, off-the-shoulder top and tight jeans, and some strappy sandal-things. She looked great.

"Thanks," I said, stepping away from my bike. "How's it going?"

"Okay. Just wondering where Zip is." Guess she wasn't waiting for me.

"Oh."

"We agreed to meet up before school," she continued smoothly, "and see if we could take you in to breakfast. Most important meal of the day, you know: got to keep you on the health-and-safety regimen. Avoid the biscuits and so-called gravy."

I was touched and flattered. "Thanks."

"You're welcome." She'd been staring into the distance, as if watching for Zip's arrival; now, however, she turned and looked at me, and offered a radiant smile. "So… heard yesterday afternoon went well."

"Yeah… seemed to." How small was this school?

"Someone from the team recorded your swim on his phone," she said, apparently seeing a confused look cross my face. "It was uploaded to YouTube last night. So even though we weren't there, at least we got to see your qualifying lap. Zip thought both the coaches were going to have heart attacks."

I tried not to glow, but failed. Sonya smiled again. "Now, don't get too puffed up with yourself, Mr Shan-the-Man. You've only been here twenty-four hours, and you're already making quite the name for yourself. Tall, good-looking, swimming star, arm candy to Kallie Corcoran…" She left the sentence hanging there, swinging gently back and forth, like something on a meat hook, but she lifted her eyebrows at me, as if requesting a confirmation or a denial.

"I don't really know Kallie," I said, trying to keep my voice steady but also — weirdly — dropping it to a quieter tone, as if someone might be listening. "She just introduced herself to me yesterday, like you guys did."

"There's a difference between introducing oneself, and *staking turf*," Sonya said dryly. "Let me guess. You going to dinner tonight at her house?"

How'd she know *that*?

Sonya laughed at my dumbstruck face. "Oh, that girl works *fast*. I'd heard stories, but this…" She shook her head with a sort of grudging admiration.

"What sort of stories?" I asked, not exactly casually.

Sonya snorted. "Mostly things about how she spent the past couple summers. Her daddy forked out a pretty penny to send her to some horse-riding camp down in Oregon for a few weeks, so she spent the past two summers doing some *heavy riding*… along with a few horses." She looked at me archly, but with a flicker of apology in her eyes. "Sorry to bust your bubble. Just thought you'd want a heads-up before you sailed right into the headwind."

"No worries," I said, feeling plenty of worries. I still hadn't had my V-card punched yet, and Kallie seemed to have a lot more experience than I did in that department.

"Who's going sailing?" Zip interjected, sauntering up, backpack slung over one shoulder. Today he was still wearing a baseball cap, but had swapped out the baseball jersey for a football one. He slipped an arm around Sonya's waist and gave her a side-hug. "Can I come?"

As what, the boat? my mind said, and I promptly hated myself for it. Why was I so obsessed with Zip's body?

"Sure, we'll use you as ballast," Sonya cracked, as Zip smacked her arm and jumped away in mock-horror. "Ouch!"

"Oh, did that hurt?" Zip looked concerned.

"Yes," Sonya mock-pouted.

"Good," Zip said, face returning to sunniness. I couldn't help but smile: they really did play off each other like a pair of sitcom pros. But now Zip was addressing me. "Hey, did Sonya tell you we want to take you in to breakfast?"

"Yeah," I said, shifting uncomfortably, because as if the gods had some sick sense of humor, right at that moment Kallie opened the front door to the school and waved at me. I waved back. Sonya and Zip turned and looked, then looked back at me.

"Ah, his master beckons," Zip intoned, as if I were some rare species in the wild beholden to a pack leader, or Queen Bee.

"Whatever you do," Sonya said, her voice dropping to an urgent whisper, "don't ask a lot of questions about her brother."

"Her brother?" I asked, confused. Kallie hadn't mentioned a brother coming to dinner. She was waving a little more emphatically now, however, and gesturing for me to come to her.

"Sshhhhh," Sonya hissed, very deliberately looking at a tree somewhere over my right shoulder, which she suddenly seemed fascinated by. "I'll tell you about it later. It's all very scandalous and sordid, and *no one's* supposed to talk about it."

"Which is why we're going to," Zip grinned devilishly. "It'll make up for her depriving you of our company during breakfast. We'll reconnoiter in Science."

"Cool," I said, bumping fists with both of them and offering an apologetic smile. "See you then." At least Sonya and Zip understood about Kallie's demands on me: that was something to be grateful for.

"Am I going to have to always compete with your...*friends*...for your attention?" Kallie asked as I hustled up to her, feeling like I'd somehow done something wrong already. She had her hair in some intricate braid pattern today, and a lace top through which you could catch a glimpse of her bra. I tried very hard not to stare at her chest, but her face was wearing an accusatory expression, which made me feel somehow ashamed and small. I had a flash of being in kindergarten and being yelled at for eating some cookies, which were supposed to be for a bake sale.

"They were telling me they saw me swim, online, last night," I said, feeling like I was somehow apologizing by offering an explanation. "You know, the one you watched in person." I don't know why I said that; I meant it to emphasize that she was there when they weren't, but now I also felt like I was the one being accusatory.

Her face looked like it had been carved out of marble — perfect ivory skin, curvy lips, devastating cheekbones, yet hard eyes. "Well — I guess that's okay," she said, looking in Sonya and Zip's direction. I turned. Sure enough, they were still watching us. Zip gave a huge wave, as if he was atop a float in a parade. Sonya raised her fingers and wiggled them, her tight smile showing no teeth.

"*Okay?* Should I get permission before I talk to other people?" I felt weirdly anxious asking this question, as though I might not like the answer.

She looked at me, and an expression of irritation crossed her face. "Oh, don't be so *silly*," she said, abruptly hitting my shoulder with her open palm. It didn't hurt — much — but it stung a little bit where the clamp for my backpack dug into my chest. "Of course you can talk to anyone you want. I just want you to want to talk to me *first*." The irritated expression melted away, and she looked wounded and a little hurt. She actually pushed out her lower lip a little bit, which only made me notice her lips even more.

"I'll try to remember to talk to you first," I said, stepping closer to her, and suddenly I was taking her chin, and holding it close. Intuitively, I knew what was going to happen next.

I don't know what I was expecting. Maybe, based on our first meeting yesterday, I thought our first kiss would be sweet and kind of gentle. But she didn't need a hint; she leaned in and kissed me, hungrily. It wasn't tentative, it didn't promise anything for the future; it demanded, possessed, it said *now*. Her tongue was suddenly sliding into my mouth, and I was so out of my mind with the pressure of her lips, her teeth knocking against mine, her chest pressed against my own, that I kind of blanked out for a few moments.

When I came back, she was pulling away from me, but she had this funny smile on her face, and she was biting her lower lip. A tiny dot of deep redness appeared there.

"What?" I said, adjusting my clothing and my posture a bit so that nothing was too obvious.

"You," she said. It was weird the way she said it, as if I were something that amused her somehow. Like a childhood toy she was appraising with some degree of fondness, but deciding whether or not to donate to the Goodwill.

"What about me?"

"I'm glad you're coming over tonight," she said, looking right at me. "Practice should be out by five, and we're a ten-minute ride from here. We eat around seven."

"What are we going to do until dinner?" I asked, a little concerned and thinking of my mom's advice.

Should I stay at practice a little longer? Would Coach Corcoran notice?

"Oh, I can think of some things," she said, a smile slowly spreading across her face, like oil on water.

"What kind of things?" I very much wanted to know, yet didn't want to know.

"I can show you my room," she said, not taking her eyes off my face, her green eyes glittering like hard little emeralds. "It's at the far end of the house. Or maybe we'll go down to the pool… and swim."

She said *swim*; that's not what she meant. I knew it. She knew it.

"Maybe," I said, my throat suddenly dry. "Um, can I— can I walk you to class?"

"I guess we should," she said languidly, as if she was doing the school a favor by showing up. "You probably don't want to skip first period on your second day here."

"No," I said, my voice almost a squeak. "I mean— we have tonight."

"Oh yes, we do," she said, running her fingers down my shirtfront and over my thigh, giving the erection straining inside my jeans a firm squeeze. I had to tense up and think of stainless-steel kitchen appliances; that's the only thing that stops the moment dead for me. Something about the cool, hard metal as the antithesis to anything warm, fleshy, or human.

She took my hand and led me through the doors into the cool darkness of *The* Jefferson Academy. I was glad that we only had about ten minutes before the first bell rang, and her Science class was at the other end of the building. I don't know what I would've done, or what she might have done to me, if we'd had more time before first period. Even though I wanted to, I was almost afraid to even think about it.

"So this is me," she said, stopping in front of the office. "I'm the front-office assistant during first period. I'll look for you at lunch?" She leaned in for another kiss.

She was an office assistant; *that's* how she got my phone number! I relaxed a little bit as I kissed her this time, knowing now that she didn't have weird supernatural powers, after all. I'd gone and worried myself over nothing, yet again.

Right?

Chapter 8

You know how, sometimes, when you break open a candy bar with a lot of caramel in it, you can pull the two halves way apart, and the caramel will *stretch, stretch, stretch,* before it breaks? That's what the morning felt like.

I had Social Studies (the Industrial Revolution, whee) and Math (Geometry, double whee) before I hit Science. I noticed Theo was in my Social Studies class. He waved a little, but he also looked a little askance when he saw me. It was a little weird after how effusive he'd been right after my qualifying swim yesterday, but I decided not to read too much into it right now. I already had enough on my mind with this strange triangle going on between me, Kallie, and Sonya and Zip. *That* would've been a fun shape to find the area and perimeter of... I wondered if Kallie would be the hypotenuse, and then had to stop thinking about it because I kept picturing her reclining along the edge of the triangle in a none-too-casual way, wearing something black and sheer and a pair of opera gloves. (I don't know where the opera gloves came from.)

When I walked into Science, Zip and Sonya were already there and waiting for me. They'd been talking as I walked in, but hushed up as I ambled to the back row and put my books down.

"Hey."

"Hey," Zip said, holding his hand up for a slap. Sonya nodded hello.

"So, what did you want to tell me about Kallie?" I asked, my voice once again dropping to a stage whisper. Why did this girl always make me feel as if at any moment I could be hauled away by covert ops, and tried for treason? If only she wasn't so great looking, and such a great kisser.

"Well, first of all," Zip stage-whispered back as roll began, "you need to tell us: is she a good kisser?"

Did Zip have ESP or telepathy?

"She's great," I said, a little gruffly.

"Oh, good," Sonya affirmed.

"Why?"

"Just being protective of you, newbie," she smiled, and patted my cheek. I'm usually cautious about people touching me, especially people I don't know very well, but she raised her hand within my eyeline, and her touch was gentle. She didn't seem to be condescending, just playful, and her concern appeared genuine.

"I don't need any help," I said, as coolly as I could, though I didn't feel very cool. My stomach was jitterbugging again.

"Not in the water, Michael Phelps," Sonya smirked.

"But on land," Zip put in helpfully, "it's good to know what you're dealing with. And Kallie Corcoran is *not* the sort of person you interact with without protection."

A wave of heat engulfed me, and I felt my face get warm. "If you're talking about sex—"

"Not *sex*," Zip said impatiently, then his eyes widened. "Not yet, I mean. Wait, have you already—?"

"No," I breathed, trying to keep calm. "I mean—"

"He means," Sonya said, one firm hand on my forearm and another on Zip's, "that you just need to know some more things about her and the family. Before…"

"Before what?"

"Before you go off swimming in the deep end of the pool," Sonya said, not meanly, but emphasizing her words just enough so I couldn't miss them.

The teacher called "Milne," and I raised my hand and said "Here," then turned back to Zip and Sonya without missing a beat. "So, what do I need to know?"

"Well, I told you about the horse riding camp," Sonya reminded me.

"Got it. What else?"

"Her family is rich," Zip said. "Like, *super* rich. Like, they have more money than God and Oprah put together. And when things get unpleasant, they use that money to make things… go away."

"Last year," Sonya murmured, opening her textbook along with the rest of the class but still keeping our conversation going, "there was some talk about some weirdness with her older brother. Like, really, weird stuff."

"What kind of weird stuff?" I felt a little more nauseous. It was probably a good thing I hadn't eaten the biscuit and gravy for breakfast.

Sonya and Zip looked at each other meaningfully. "Her brother, Eddie," Zip muttered. "He came out to the family two years ago."

"So?"

"So," Sonya continued smoothly, "he was supposedly seeing somebody from the swim team. Do you know a good looking blond boy named Theo?"

Something clicked in my brain. *That* was why he was looking at me weirdly before the locker room and in class that morning; his demeanor had changed once Kallie came over to me after my swim.

I must have had a funny expression, because Zip said, "Aha. Exactly."

"Theo told a friend," Sonya continued, "that Eddie had some issues. The whole *family* has issues."

"Like what?" I wasn't sure what exactly this had to do with Kallie, but I was intrigued.

"Swords and weapons," Sonya said. "All over the house. Eddie was obsessed with them, and so's their dad."

"They go on these trippy survivalist weekends," Zip added helpfully. "Take bows and arrows and a whole bunch of guns, and go 'live off the land' for a couple days. They'd only eat what they'd hunt, and in their spare time they'd do target practice. Both Eddie and Kallie know how to use a crossbow, a rifle, a Glock, and who knows what else."

"So what's wrong with that?" I said, trying not to sound defensive. "Lots of people know how to shoot. It's probably better than just sitting around and doing video game versions of using weapons."

"Hey, I resent that remark," Zip said. "In the online world, I'm like Legolas."

"Yes," Sonya said acidly, "and my avatar online is Beyonce. Meanwhile, back in the real world…"

"So, what else is wrong with Eddie, besides he and Kallie liking weapons?" I continued, a little impatiently.

"There's a rumor," Zip said, his voice dropping to barely a whisper, "that he didn't want to be gay, and that he broke up with Theo after having some sort of weird psychotic breakdown. Kallie was ringside for most of that."

"And there was also a rumor that someone in that house later caught him doing something really nasty with a jar of peanut butter and the family dog," Sonya murmured, her lips barely moving.

"Eeewwwww!" This burst out of me without warning, and the entire class looked at me, including Mr Farthing. I blushed like a beet.

"There's something stuck to the back page of Shan's textbook," Sonya called out to the room. Zip jumped up and grabbed a sanitary wipe, and started scrubbing at the nonexistent dried mucus or God-knows-what-else in my book, putting on a good show.

"So anyways," Zip muttered, "we just wanted to make sure that you knew some background. Eddie is supposed to be at Evergreen State, but he flunked out and now just lives at home and takes community college credit here and there. So be warned if you see him at dinner."

"Yeah," I said. "Especially if they serve hot dogs or peanut butter."

Sonya let out a snort-laugh that made her choke, and she left the room to get water, wiping her eyes and goosing me in the ribs on her way out. Her touch wasn't anything like the way Kallie acted towards me, and I wondered for a split second what it would be like to have Sonya as a girlfriend. Then again, I was already wondering what tonight would bring me with Kallie; trying to imagine myself with a *second* girl was pretty much beyond my wildest comprehension.

I just hoped I wouldn't be seeing Eddie that night for dinner.

Chapter 9

"You like?" Kallie said, turning off the ignition and smiling at me. I was too busy trying to remember to close my mouth to answer her.

Like was not the word. The house sat atop a rising lawn that sloped down to the street and was ringed with a gazillion different flowers and shrubs. The driveway turned as it rose, and the garage was to the left; the house itself looked like one of those faux-Medieval castles, redone as a ten-or-twelve-room chateau that mashes up French and American architecture. The bricks were deep reddish-gray, the trim was gold and burgundy, and there was actually a middle-aged butler in a uniform opening the front door and coming down the stairs to us.

Kallie got out of the car and walked around, tossing the keys to him. "Parsons, this is Shan. Give him your best service."

"Yes, Miss Kallie," the butler said, bowing to her and then nodding politely to me, holding the door open and extending a hand in case I needed it, getting out of the front seat. Without thinking, I took it, feeling like some sort of royalty getting out of a carriage instead of just a high-school guy getting out of a really nice Beamer. I nodded back, unsure what to do next.

"This way," Kallie called airily, gesturing, as Parsons slid into the front seat and opened the garage door. Apparently, parking her car was one of his regular duties. I caught a glimpse of the garage's interior, with spaces for four cars: it was as gleaming and immaculate as a showroom, complete with a white Mercedes convertible and a silver Lexus minivan. Kallie's car was dark blue, and also a convertible with a gray interior. My mind flashed briefly on my battered bike chained up back at school, the same one I'd had since my mom had bought it for me almost five years ago, as I followed Kallie up the steps and into the house.

For me, the lobby of The Excelsior is pretty much the definition of high-end living, and that's a hotel. This house's foyer was even more elegant and high-end than the Excelsior, because it was newer and it wasn't designed to get you to stay there as a guest. Kallie and her family actually *lived* here, amidst the giant glass table with the huge flower arrangement, the tiled floor, the antique rifles on the walls, the gilt trim, the curved stairs that disappeared behind a glittering chandelier. I had a momentary flash of my grandmother in her tiny yellow kitchen when I was a little boy, rolling out biscuit dough and softly singing to me, *"I'll build a stairway to paradise..."* I always thought she meant heaven; maybe she just meant the second floor of a house like this.

We went through a doorway and an enormous room filled with chairs, a giant-screen TV, a pool table, and brown leather furniture that looked like it would swallow you if you sat on it. Ancient Japanese swords and samurai memorabilia hung on the walls, giving the room an intimidating feeling. Kallie walked with a smooth stride, not even bothering to point anything out; this was her life, welcome to it. A somewhat demanding tone came into her voice, oddly cooler than when she spoke to Parsons: "Mom? Mother?"

Then we were in a kitchen big enough that, if you were trying to cook Thanksgiving for sixteen or so, you'd need roller skates to get around and get everything done. A tiny Filipino woman was at the stove, seemingly taking care of four different bubbling pots simultaneously. A black-haired woman who looked like Kallie, only more elegantly dressed in a dark-purple pantsuit, was sitting at the table, balefully eyeing a hand-drawn menu. As we came in, she took off her glasses and smiled at us.

"Hello, darling," she said, carefully turning one cheek so that Kallie could air-kiss right next to it. She said it as if she were some sort of European supermodel, with a kind of blasé quality underneath the affectionate words. I noticed that Kallie had some of her mother's speech patterns, only higher-pitched.

"Mother, this… is Shan," Kallie said, turning and gesturing to me as if I were a new car on "The Price is Right." I wondered if I should have worn a shiny dark blue exterior, and gray seats. "Shan, this is my mom, Lara."

"Oh, *hello*," Lara said, extending one perfectly dressed arm straight from the Chico's ad. Her nails were perfectly manicured and the color of cranberries. "You're the swimmer I told Kallie to watch for. My, I'm glad she took my advice."

"Thank you, ma'am," I said, trying to keep my voice steady and remembering my manners. "You have a beautiful home." My mom would've been so proud of me.

"Oh *thank* you," she said, smiling slowly, still looking at me. "We like it." (Does *we* include Eddie-who-is-hopefully-caged-somewhere?) A slight shadow crossed her face as she looked behind me. "Kallie, what are you eating?"

Kallie had grabbed a bunch of grapes and a small bowl, and was pulling a couple off plump green globules off the branches and popping them in her mouth. "Grapes."

"Darling, we're having dinner in an hour and half," Mrs Corcoran said in a gently chiding tone, as if the words were dusted with a sprinkling of snow. "And it's going to be a roast. Don't fill up."

"We won't," Kallie said in a bored way. "Seven is an eternity from now. We'll take these upstairs, and Shan will help me eat them, won't you?"

"Sure," I said, not knowing if I was supposed to take her side or her mom's in this discussion. But her mom pursed her lips into a kind of knowing smile, and I figured I was doing okay. "It was very nice meeting you, Mrs Corcoran," I said, offering a little wave, not really knowing what else to do.

"Oh, Lara," she said chidingly. "And thank you for helping her with the grapes. We're trying to keep her from going overboard with sweets and treats."

"It's fruit, mother, not a banana split," Kallie said with a slight edge to her voice as she tilted her head towards the exit, indicating that I should follow her.

"Nonetheless," her mother returned absently, already looking at the dinner menu again, her voice drifting way up towards the ceiling.

The carpet was plush and soft under my feet as we made our way upstairs, down a hallway, turned, then went down another hallway. Kallie apparently had her own wing in the house. I decided to play dumb and do a little fishing. "Is all this for you?"

"Me and my brother," she said, still walking. "He graduated a couple years ago and now takes various classes here and there. We won't see him tonight."

I felt a wave of relief and my body uncoiling as tension drained out of it. I wasn't going to have to deal with something I wasn't prepared for after all. Then Kallie said, "Here we are," and I was in her room.

I don't know what I expected — well, yes, I kind of did. I'd been expecting something vibrant and sensual, with little bursts of color, like Kallie herself. Her room was almost spartan, with a simple dark bedspread and crimson sheets peeking out. The bed was huge and old-fashioned, with a giant headboard and four posts at the corners. The walls were a dusty-rose color, and the wood trim and the windows, which were closed very decisively against the warm afternoon sun, were blocked by dark crimson drapes with black fringe. She had an ancient-looking desk with a laptop on it, and a bulletin board housing a few notes and photos; one of them showed her doing a selfie with a dark-haired guy who could have been her twin, except for his wiry body and ocean-blue eyes and a mocking mouth. That and the laptop were the most modern things in the room; everything else gave the impression someone much, much older lived here.

"Ta-daaa. What do you think?" Kallie asked, in a bored voice that implied it didn't matter much what I thought.

"I like it," I said, not sure if I was lying or not. "It's— very adult."

"Adult," she repeated, smiling at me as she shifted her gaze sideways, using her peripheral vision. "Haven't heard that before."

"Well, I mean…" I had no idea what I meant. "It's not like a lot of other teenagers' rooms I've seen."

"What's your room like?" she asked, sliding onto the bedspread and indicating that I should take a seat on the floor on a very thick, faux-fur throw rug.

"I dunno. Guy's room. Music and sports posters, dirty clothes."

"That's all?" She was fixing me with that penetrating gaze again, the one that made me simultaneously turned on and jittery.

I shrugged. "I'm not very interesting."

(I didn't want to go into the whole thing about my past at that point: Frankie, the breakup, the year of moving and hiding, the changing schools, Frankie tracking down my mom, hiding again at the Excelsior, the cops, the ending. It'd probably come out sooner or later. For now, I just wanted to enjoy the fact that Kallie thought I was the kind of guy who belonged in her house, in this room.)

"You think?" she asked, plucking off another grape and offering it to me, putting it in my mouth and letting her fingers trace over my lips for a moment. The pressure of her fingertips caused a trickle of sweat to run down the back of my neck.

"I know."

"What else do you do, besides swim?"

"Nothing," I said. "I mean, I dunno. Watch TV, sometimes play video games. Tool around on my bike. Help my mom around the house."

"Your *mom*," Kallie said, rolling the word around in her mouth, tasting it. "She works at the Excelsior, right?"

"Have you been looking at my student file?" I asked her, a little more accusatory than I meant to.

Most girls, when confronted with something like that, you would've expected them to shrink away, or giggle, or be nervous. Kallie just smiled, very slowly, running her finger over her bedspread as though it were a Persian cat, and she was the villain in a James Bond movie. Neither of us spoke for a few seconds, though there was enough electricity in the room to power the Space Needle.

Finally, she said very lightly, "I like to know some things about somebody before I date them."

"Do I get to ask you things?" I returned, again getting that nervous-excited feeling. I was giving my all not to get too turned on by the fact that I was sitting on the floor in her bedroom, looking up at her, and the warm, dimly lit room had that same exotic, vanilla smell she'd worn yesterday — God! Yesterday morning.

"It depends," she said cagily, looking deep into my eyes. "How would you like to come join me up here, and we can talk some more?"

Pinpricks of more sweat broke out on my neck and armpits. I tried to keep my voice steady: "If I come up there, I don't know how much talking we're going to do."

"Exactly."

I took the bowl of denuded branches and set it on her nightstand, stood up, and climbed onto her bed and slid my body down next to hers. She rolled over and looked at me, her eyes boring into my skull, as she ran her fingers around my collarbone, my neck, the back of my head. She loosened my tie, pulled it off. "Let's let our bodies do the talking."

I didn't complain. I pressed my lips against hers, letting her tongue slide expertly into my mouth and caress my teeth. Her hands went down my back and were suddenly under my shirt, pulling it out and untucking it. I could feel every muscle in my back, worked out from thousands of hours in pools, suddenly coming to life and tingling under her touch. Her nails raked gently against my skin, then a little harder. Every part of me felt like it was popping and crackling under the skin, a fireworks stand going off one fizzy sparkler at a time, but always continuing to build.

I was wearing my nice dress shirt — the only one I had — and she had the buttons open and the shirt slid off of me so artfully, I didn't even realize it was gone until I felt her teeth scrape against my bare skin. I was very glad that her room was a second floor and a couple of hallways away from anyone who might have been listening.

I was completely outside of myself. Whomever Shan Milne was inside, the scared, scrawny little kid with the dirty face and the tiny, skinny body, was being obliterated, one exploding cell at a time. I was so feverishly hot I felt like I might set her bedspread on fire, then I was shivering as if wracked by chills. I could hear myself making strange, indecent sounds which I'd never permitted myself to make over the past five years, not even when at home alone in the privacy of my bedroom. Yet Kallie, aside from the occasional sigh of exertion as she rearranged her body into some new position to kiss or lick me, didn't say anything. There was only the sound of her lips against my flesh.

I was dimly aware that my clothes had been removed by this point, that her tongue was now moving all over my body. I didn't think I could ever feel this good, and then her tongue went further south. If I'd stopped to listen to myself, if I could've seen myself, I would've been embarrassed beyond words. But I didn't, so I wasn't.

And then, just as I thought it was all I ever could have hoped for, I heard the click. Felt my arms being pulled up, locked in place. Felt the handcuffs pull and tighten around the headboard post, and the metal bite into my wrists.

What the—

Something was next to my face. My underwear. Then her lips again, kissing and nibbling on my ear, her breath warm, her sweater removed at last so I could feel her breasts against my cheek. I opened my mouth to kiss her, and instead felt my briefs being stuffed into it.

Jesus! What was going on?

Part of me was frightened now, but the rest of me was buckled in until the ride came to a complete stop. Kallie straddled my torso, her face an impenetrable mask, except for a small smile. In the dim light, I watched her scoot her body down, rearrange herself yet again, and go to work once more with her tongue, making me whimper. She did such a good job that I didn't even hear the drawer next to the bed slowly being opened.

Then I felt the pain.

Oh God, oh God, oh *fuck,* the pain!

It was like being ripped in half. I think I tried to scream, and I understood why Kallie had done what she did with the cuffs and my underwear. Those two things were now the only things holding me in place, and preventing me from yelling myself hoarse.

Through it all, in the gathering darkness and the heat, I felt her body rising and falling with my own. She was straddling me now, letting her weight fall forward and using it to hold me down, her dark hair covering my face like something devouring me, her nails digging into my wrists. The bed was creaking under our weight, and there was wetness on my cheeks — from sweat or tears, I didn't know any more.

She was in my ear again, whispering insistently, "Come on. Come on, you bad boy… Yeah, come on you *dirty,* bad boy… Give it up for me. Give it up for me… Right there…" Her voice dropped to a near-hiss. "Oh yeah. Oh yeah, oh yeah, oh yeeaahhh…"

I bucked once, twice, three times, four times, feeling the orgasm burst out of me like King Kong tearing his way through New York. I bit down hard so I didn't yell or cry out. I didn't feel amazing any more, like I had just a few brief minutes ago. I felt hot and dirty, spent and used. Beyond those emotions, the rest of my mind was a black void.

So. That was sex. That was my first time, never to be forgotten — not even if I someday wanted to.

I closed my eyes, too ashamed to watch the after-process, as whatever-it-was was slid out of me — oh Jesus God, the feeling of release, and I tried not to lose complete control of my bowels on the spot. The *click* as the cufflinks were undone. The sound of the door opening; then, in the distance, running water. Then the *click* as the door closed again, and the warm washcloth being run all over me, cleaning me up, like a baby being changed.

I opened my eyes. I had never, in all of my years in a locker room, felt so naked, so exposed. My wrists had red marks were the cuffs were, and I couldn't describe the soreness elsewhere.

I sat there, naked and wet and bruised, on her bed, watching as she tossed back her hair, rearranged her sweater, adjusted her skirt, stood up, smoothing her outfit back to what it was. Perfect.

She came close, handed me my shirt from the bedpost, bent close to kiss my cheek, and without thinking, for just a second, I recoiled. I didn't want her kissing me at that moment. I wanted to go home. I wanted my mom.

She pulled back and surveyed me curiously, the way a scientist looks at an unfamiliar specimen. "You did really well for a first timer," she said, not unkindly. "I think we both came at the same time."

I locked my eyes on the rug, as my vision of it started to blur and waver. I pulled my shirt in front of me to cover myself. My head was throbbing, and I felt dizzy and nauseous. How in the name of God was I supposed to eat after this?

"I'll be downstairs helping set the table," she said, as if giving me instructions on in war games. "You go ahead and get your clothes on. Use the bathroom across the hall, and wash your face and comb your hair. There are spare brushes in the top drawer. Just fix yourself up nice before dinner, get your tie just right, make a good impression on my dad. Mm-kay?"

"Do you seriously expect me to just— make *small talk* with your family now?" I said, my voice not much more than a quavering whisper. My lungs, my championship lungs that allowed me to swim for uninterrupted meters at a time, now seemed to be full of sludge. I felt as if I were drowning in a mountain pool of bone-crushingly cold, deep, green water.

"Of course you will," Kallie said, very simply. "My uncle is your coach, remember? You're going to be a swimming star at Jefferson. It'll all be fine." She looked at me with what seemed to be a fond smile, but the shadows had grown in the room, and her eyes were now hooded. I couldn't see if they showed any emotion. "And the roast'll be delicious. Lupita will see to that."

She came near me again, gently kissed my cheek, and left, closing the door behind her. I sat naked in the gloom, in a strange bedroom, in a strange house, staring at the rug for a while, until my eyes blurred.

Then I slowly, painfully, began to get dressed.

Chapter 10

I don't think, since Jesus celebrated the Last Supper, has there been a more torturous meal.

Just as Zip and Sonya said, the dining room also had a variety of weapons affixed to the walls, similar to the TV room. Here, however, the weapons seemed more medieval: I noticed a couple of rapiers crossed over the entryway, and a broadsword or two mounted on the walls. There were even a couple of fierce-looking crossbows hung up, arrows still in quivers next to them. The room had the feel of a hunting lodge. I had no idea any more if I was the hunter or the prey.

I was seated next to Kallie, of course, and was trying very hard the entire meal not to make overt eye contact with her. For her part, Kallie was acting with extreme delicacy — ever-so-gently touching my arm, my hand, as she passed the dishes, the way you might when you're trying to soothe a snappish animal, or a cranky child. I was hyper-aware of her touch; I was also aware of the tenderness every time I shifted in the hard, formal dining room chair, and the feeling of rawness at my wrists, buttoned-up securely beneath my dress shirt.

Everything looked perfectly normal, yet nothing was.

Lara was still wearing the pantsuit from earlier. Kallie's father, John, had one of those beefy, English faces, the kind that always looks a little pink and sweaty, and he wore a blue shirt in a hue that resembled Kallie's sweater. Coach Corcoran, of course, I knew, having just seen him two hours— God! Only two hours ago at practice. He was the only one who was casual enough to wear shorts and a melon-colored polo shirt. He was Kallie's mother's brother, and I saw where the dark hair came from in their family.

I chewed the roast. I chewed the vegetables. I skipped the bread. I stared at the formal dinnerware with the gold band around the edge of the plates, thinking of the all-purpose chipped pasta bowls that my mother and I ate out of most nights, the same ones we'd had for years. I didn't taste anything.

When the conversation washed over me, it was like being surprised by a blast of freezing surf.

"Well, Shan," Coach was saying now, as he tucked into a forkful of scalloped potatoes, "how do you think this afternoon went?"

I was, for an instant, so completely thrown that I butterfingered my fork, and it clattered to the plate. I might have gasped a little before I remembered: swim practice. My voice sounded like a rusty hinge. "I... I think it went okay."

"Okay?" Coach boomed, turning to Kallie's parents, as Kallie again laid a none-too-subtle squeeze on my arm. "This boy is part seal! He's only on his second day with us, and already he's got several school records in his sights. We're lucky to have him."

"Yes," Lara said, nodding approvingly at me, "he seems like quite a desirable boy. At least, Kallie seems to think so."

"Mother, please," Kallie said, her voice coming out hard and clipped, as if she were issuing a warning.

"What? He seems like a very nice boy, and you seem to like him very much. That's perfectly obvious," Lara said, reaching for a glass of wine. She shot Kallie an appraising glance, as if daring her to ramp up the argument.

"So, Shan," John said, slicing his roast into an assortment of blood-red pieces, "your mother works at The Excelsior, I hear?"

Had they been talking about me before I came down for dinner? "Yes, sir."

"That's a good place," he said, looking at me carefully, as if I was supposed to agree with him. It was the same look Kallie used. "I've had lunch at Catch a couple times."

"Oh, yes!" Coach interjected. "That's the place that does the great fish-and-chips, with the Panko bread crumbs."

"No, the Panko is over at Mulligan's," John said dismissively. "Catch does beer batter."

"I think you're wrong," Coach said, almost playfully. He seemed to enjoy needling Kallie's dad.

"Bet you lunch," John returned, as if volleying a tennis ball over the net.

I was having a complete out-of-body experience. Here we all were, talking idly about what's the best local seafood. Here's the girl who wanted to be my girlfriend, showing me off to her parents and my coach. Not forty-five minutes earlier, she and I had been punching my V-card (emphasis on *punch*) upstairs in her room, and now I could barely get food down.

The room felt stuffy and humid, and Kallie kept touching my arm. I didn't want to be touched any more. I didn't want to talk about seafood. I wanted to be biking home in the dusky twilight, headphones on, drowning out the rest of the world. I wanted to be lying at the bottom of a swimming pool, staring up at the world through the cool, shimmering azure water. I wanted time and space to process everything.

I suddenly realized Lara — Mrs Corcoran — was talking to me, and I was so zoned out I wasn't paying attention. "Pardon me?"

"I said, what do you think of The Jefferson Academy so far?"

"It's great," I said, putting on my Good-Boy Face and Voice. "The classes are really interesting, and kids seem really… awesome."

"I need to introduce him to some people," Kallie said warmly, as if I was a little kid and she was going to tuck me in with milk and cookies. "He needs to make some *normal* friends. He got sucked into hanging out with a couple of non-cons the past two days."

"Non-cons?" Coach asked, her brow furrowing. I was glad he did. I didn't know what she meant, either.

"Non-conformists," Kallie said, an edge of distaste in her voice. "Losers. That black girl with the bad attitude, and that *thing* — that fat, Jewish he-she."

BLAMMO. That was the sound of my mind silently exploding like the Death Star, as I suddenly realized what it was about Zip that I'd never quite understood, and why I'd felt slightly uncomfortable around her. Him. My brain swam… I suddenly realized I didn't know who Zip really was.

"He-she?" Kallie's dad stopped chewing and stared at her, as though he'd taken a bite of something distasteful. Lara's eyebrows were so raised, they looked like they were going to crawl off her forehead.

"They say she used to be a girl," Kallie said urgently, as though warning us all about some sort of spreading plague, "but then, around second grade, she cut her hair short and started wearing boys' clothes. Now that's all she does — wears boys' athletic gear and baseball hats. And everyone goes along with it!"

"I know who you're talking about," Coach said, unexpectedly. "We got a memo about it, start of the year. We're supposed to treat him as if he were a boy, and let him change in the restroom stall."

"But she *isn't* a boy!" Kallie's face, unlike her father's, didn't get pink when she was worked up; it became even paler and deathlier white. She barely looked like she had any blood running through her at all.

"Tell that to the parents," Coach said, heavily. "They threatened to sue the school if we didn't go along with it. Apparently, this *kid* takes hormones, and is planning on having her breasts removed in the next couple years, after graduation. Until then, we all have to play ball." He let out a grim kind of chuckle. "No pun intended."

"Those poor parents," Kallie's mom sighed, fingers toying with her wine glass.

"*Anyways,*" Kallie went on, dragging the conversation back on track as if trying to turn an ocean liner, "I'm going to introduce Shan to some *quality* peeps." She smiled at me benevolently. I didn't know what to say to that, so I just stared at her, thinking, *why would she think Sonya had a bad attitude? Or was it just that Sonya didn't take any crap?*

"There are some good guys on the swim team," Coach put in. "Nice kids; a lot of them I've worked with for a couple years. Shan, anyone you think you're hitting it off with?"

I must have lost my mind at that moment, or maybe I was curious to see their reactions. Maybe I was secretly ticked off that they'd been ragging on Sonya and Zip, who'd been nothing but nice to me. Maybe I was still mentally screwed-up from earlier. Maybe it was the fact that Eddie wasn't there, so I felt somewhat safe. But all too innocently, I said, "Theo seems really nice."

It was as if I'd put a foot through a stained-glass window. Lara actually dropped her silverware and turned pale; James lowered his glass, and looked for a moment like he was going to turn into the Wolfman. Coach Corcoran dropped his gaze and stirred the remainder of his food, sopping up some juice from the meat.

In the ensuing pause, Kallie took my hand and squeezed it in such a way that it looked like she was just being friendly, but I felt her nails dig into my palm. Her eyes were too bright to look at squarely, so I used my peripheral vision. Her voice sounded far away.

"Oh, I'd stay away from him, too."

"Why?" I asked, squeezing back, and looking at her full-on. I felt a pang of something in my chest. Fear? Excitement? Power? For perhaps the first time since meeting her, it seemed like I had the upper hand.

"He lies," she said, pointedly. I'm not kidding when I say pointedly; it's like her words were knitting needles, and she wanted to stab something with them.

"What about?" I was trying to maintain the innocent façade, but she was looking at me like she was trying to decipher what I was up to, and I felt a wave of nerves overcome me.

"He's just not a very... good person," Lara said unexpectedly. She looked somewhere between nauseous and furious, and was staring at her husband as though they were communicating telepathically.

"He's a great swimmer," Coach said unenthusiastically, shoveling his food in. He looked like he was looking forward to dinner being over, too.

"No one said he wasn't," James said, his eyes flicking around the table. His voice was struggling to be cool, but there seemed to be a lot of emotion seething under it. "He's a great athlete. He and our son Eddie— were very close for a time. We just thought he was one thing, and…"

"And he was another," Kallie said warningly, eyes glittering. "Kind of a wolf in sheep's clothing. So, watch out for him, too."

"I don't know who's going to be left that I can talk to," I joked, trying to be light, but underneath I was completely serious. It was only my second day at this school, and I'd just basically been warned away from three of the people who'd been nicest to me.

Was I a sheep, too?

"I *told* you," Kallie said, a touch of irritation in her voice, "I'll take care of you. I'll introduce you around tomorrow. Just don't tell people about— what we've been discussing."

"What have we been discussing?" I asked, deliberately playing dumb.

"People you don't need to know," she said, airily. "I mean, I know you want to fit in at the Academy, and do well at swimming, and get good grades…" Everyone was looking at me now, as though I were a Rubik's cube they couldn't solve.

Kallie went on, her voice now reassuring and soothing again. "Shan, you deserve good things to happen to you. We can *make* those things happen. We can help you — if you let us."

Everyone was nodding now, looking at me, and I felt my stomach lurch from the pressure. I knew if I didn't get to a bathroom in the next few seconds, I was going to regret it. Mumbling, "Excuse me," I threw my napkin on the table and ran for the rest room. As I left, I heard Lara say, "Oh, how *cute* — he's choked up!"

I wasn't choked up. I felt like I might throw up; there's a big difference.

In the bathroom, I splashed some cold water on my face and took a seat on the toilet, trying to collect my thoughts as they whizzed around me like angry yellowjackets. Everyone seemed nice — well, they said nice things, but then they said hurtful, cruel things. Everyone seemed interested in me, wanted to help me. Why did I feel like I was being pressured? Why couldn't I be more grateful for these opportunities they were presenting — opportunities which could help not only me, but my mom, too?

And why was it so hard for me to say *No* to Kallie? Earlier, in her bedroom… I got the shivers just replaying it in my mind. Could I have fought harder, really truly said *'No!'*? At dinner, should I have defended Zip and

Sonya, even Theo, more? Why couldn't I stand up for myself?

Because I'm really a loser.

That was the God's-honest truth, and it came to me sitting in a powder-blue and peach bathroom, with seashells on the shower curtain and scattered about, just so, on the counter next to the sink.

I was. I was a loser. I was a kid from a broken home, whose dad had skipped town just after I was born. I was a kid who'd been regularly smacked around for almost five years by Frankie. I was a kid who'd gone into hiding with his mom, using aliases and changing schools for an additional set of years, until Frankie finally succumbed to cancer before finding us. I was a kid who consequently could barely catch a ball, sink a basket, sing on key, and due to my haphazard education, was still struggling with reading, writing, and math.

All I could do was swim, and say, "Yes."

For the second time that evening, things in front of me — in this case, delicate little shell-shaped soaps — blurred.

Surprisingly, Kallie decided not to drive me back to school.

"I've got homework to do," she said, as we stood aimlessly by the front door with the rest of her family, "and a list to make of people to introduce you to tomorrow. Uncle Jack will drive you back to get your bike."

I didn't know why she was pawning me off on her uncle, but I was, momentarily, grateful. I was afraid, if we were alone together, she was going to start running her hand over my thigh or something like that, and then God knew where or how we'd wind up. I still wasn't sure how to say "No" to her.

I kissed her, almost perfunctorily, just long enough to linger. Her lips had a trace of butterscotch on them from dessert and tasted delicious, like something sweet that you know isn't good for you, but it's so hard to stop after the first bite. Her mom said "Awwwww," and her dad cleared his throat. I shook both of their hands and thanked them for dinner.

In the car, Coach didn't talk much. Thank God school was only ten minutes away. He did say, "Did you enjoy yourself?"

"Yeah," I said. "It was cool."

"You did great," he said. "My sister's husband is quite a piece of work. My sister is quite a piece of work." He chuckled. "Hell, *everyone* in that house is a piece of work. But you definitely brought the A-game."

"I wanted everyone to like me," I said, honestly. It came out much quieter than I'd meant it to.

"They did," he said, flicking on his turn signals. There was a pause for a moment. "But son, remember, it's early in the game. You're still settling in. Don't worry too much about everyone liking you; just be your best self. Then people will."

I didn't know what my "best self" was. That was the problem. "Okay."

The lights were still ablaze at school as the night custodians worked their magic. Coach dropped me off at the bike rack, and I slammed the car door and waved as he pulled away. It was only eight thirty, and in Seattle it stays light in the late summer for quite a while.

I stood next to the bike rack, staring at the pink-streaked sky, thinking about the fact that I was now supposedly A Man. In fact, I couldn't remember the last time I felt more like a little boy.

"Shan!" The voice startled me, and I jumped a little. Sonya stepped out of the shadows, book bag slung over her arm, headphones dangling from her ear.

"What are you doing here?" I asked, confused.

"I forgot my math book," she said, holding up the tome. "I could download Science off the website, or do English via Spark Notes, but there was no way I was going to let math slide. We already have a quiz scheduled for this Friday."

"Did you get dropped off?"

"I walked. I only live about a mile away; it's barely a few songs on Spotify," she said, laughing. She took a step towards me, looked carefully at my face, and stopped laughing. "So…how was dinner?"

I smiled, shook my head. Then I started laughing silently, then I kept laughing, and then, all of a sudden, I wasn't laughing any more.

We stood there, in the evening light, one spotlight from the streetlamp shining on us, and she put her arms around me and held me close, and stroked my hair while — just for a moment — I cried.

Chapter 11

"This," Zip said, holding up a forkful of Hawaiian omelet with long, ropey strands of cheese that stretched all the way from his fork down to his plateful of eggs, hash browns and slabs of toast, "is the best egg dish I think I've ever eaten in my life."

"Better than your bubbe's eggs, lox and onions?" Sonya asked playfully, sipping her green tea. She'd already finished her blueberry pancakes.

"Do *not* impugn my bubbe," Zip said, in such a formal way, I couldn't help but snicker. "And certainly do not impugn her cooking. I'll have you know, she smuggled her recipes out of Eastern Europe right past the Communists *and* the Nazis."

"*Oy*, the guilt," Sonya said, smacking her forehead.

"These are, however," Zip went on, ignoring her and addressing me, "possibly the best eggs *as eggs* I can remember eating. Eggs, lox and onions are an entirely different thing, especially if matzo gets involved."

"Did you suggest we have breakfast just so we can discuss eggs and suffering in the Old Country?" I asked, using a playful tone to disguise the seriousness of my question. It was Thursday morning, and after my brief crying jag before I'd walked Sonya home last night to her Tudor-style house (her father was a neurosurgeon), she told me that she was calling Zip, and we were going to have our delayed breakfast this morning, and talk. ("Not negotiable," she said coolly, when I tried to beg off.)

Trying to come up with a place Kallie wouldn't see us, of course, necessitated it being away from school. I'd thus suggested we meet at The Excelsior, which was 1) a quick trip to campus when we were done; 2) cheap, due to my mom's discount, and 3) a chance for my mom to meet Sonya and Zip.

When I'd walked in the door last night, she was sitting in front of the TV wearing an old football jersey and sweatpants, finishing a glass of wine and laughing her head off at an old *Friends* rerun. (Is there anything sadder than sitting alone while watching a sitcom called *Friends*?) She'd wanted to hear all about dinner, but after having rehashed it with Sonya, and it being after ten o'clock, all I wanted to do was go to sleep and recharge, and not think.

"But can't you just tell me a *little* bit about it? How was the food?"

"Mom, *no.* I'm tired, and I just want to go to bed. Okay?" I was already backing out of the living room and unbuttoning my shirt, trying to avoid flashbacks to Kallie's bedroom.

"I'd just like to meet some of the people you're getting to be friends with," she said, a little wistfully.

"Do you think maybe I should call up Kallie's mom, and introduce myself?"

"Why don't I have Sonya and Zip meet me for breakfast tomorrow, when you're working at the coffee shop?" I hurriedly countered. "I'll drive your car to school, then pick you up late afternoon." Given the choices, I figured having her meet The Mad Tea Party was safer than having her meet the Addams Family. (I had no proof that Mr and Mrs Corcoran had versions of Thing or Cousin It running around their house, but after the previous five hours, I wasn't assuming anything any more.)

And it actually worked out handily. I texted Sonya, who texted Zip. I had to get up early to drive in with my mom, but she started her shift at six-thirty, and Sonya and Zip agreed to meet me at seven, so we could have a leisurely meal before school bells started ringing at eight fifteen.

I realized that morning that I'd barely eaten at the Corcorans, and with my swimming regimen and my metabolism, I was actually almost weak with hunger and suffering a serious headache. A double-mocha from the espresso bar, and a plateful of *real* biscuits and gravy (not school cafeteria versions), and I was feeling semi-human again, despite the smell of green peppers sizzling in the air. I don't like peppers.

But now Sonya put her mug down and folded her hands, resting her chin on her fingers, and looked at me directly, Zip mirroring her gaze even as he kept shoveling omelet and potatoes in.

"We," Sonya began, a little formally, "have only known you a couple days. So what we have to say, you can take with as much salt as you want."

"The whole pillar, if necessary," Zip said helpfully, scrambling metaphors like the eggs. Sonya elbowed him.

"Okay…" I said, cautiously. I was ninety-nine point nine per cent sure I knew where this was going.

"The thing is," Zip said, "you seem like an awesome guy. Like, really awesome. And our school doesn't have a lot of those."

"We have a surplus of rich, white pricks," Sonya said flatly; so flatly, it was as if the words had been stepped on by a herd of elephants. "There are only so many really good people out there, and we think you're one of them."

"And we want to keep you all for ourselves," Zip cracked. Sonya gently, but firmly, touched his arm, then my hand.

"No, we don't," Sonya corrected. "We want you to have what *you* want. But it has come to our attention that Kallie seems to… definitely be, well…"

"How's everyone doing?" My mom was suddenly standing by the table, coffee pot in one hand and hot water in the other, making her voice equally warm and inviting. I hated noticing, but I was happy that she looked really pretty this morning. Her uniform had been washed and starched over the weekend, so it was still holding up; she'd taken two minutes to put on some makeup, and was wearing the emerald-studded earrings my grandparents and I had given her a couple Christmases ago. "Zip? Sonya? Need a top-off? My boy needs his rocket fuel first thing in the morning." She laughed a little, and I didn't care that she was teasing me because she looked so nice and happy, and she was so excited to meet Sonya and Zip. They seemed to like her, too.

"I'd love some more," Zip said, angling his mug. "Thank you." His manners were exquisite.

"You're welcome," my mom smiled. "Thank you for taking such good care of Shan and helping him settle in. I feel good knowing he's met nice guys like you."

"Mom…" Okay, now she was pushing it.

"I'm going," she laughed, pouring a quick splash of water into Sonya's tea. "And guys, breakfast is on me today. Don't worry about it." She took Sonya's and my empty plates as she left. Zip was still snorkeling his bounty.

"She's so nice," Sonya said, a note of awe in her voice.

"She really is," Zip nodded through his potatoes.

"Yeah, well." I shrugged.

"No," Sonya said, "you're nice, too. I see where you get it from."

"Anyhoo," Zip said, "Kallie. We just want to make sure you know what you're getting into, because it sounds as if last night you had some… reservations."

"How much did you tell him?" I asked Sonya, trying not to let my voice carry, as my mom welcomed a new couple into a booth a few feet away and handed them menus.

"Just enough." Sonya's face didn't reveal anything. I had a weird flash of Kallie's face last night, before she'd gone downstairs. Were girls always this impenetrable? Then again, I hadn't shared *every* detail of my encounter in Kallie's room with Sonya; just enough to imply that it had kind of fried my brain, and I didn't know how to feel about it. I felt guilty for not being completely honest, but I was also not comfortable being completely candid.

Then again…

"Well," I said, folding my hands, and looking at Zip directly, "maybe we both need to be honest with each other."

"Meaning?" Zip looked momentarily thrown. Sonya narrowed her eyes, trying to figure out where I was going with this.

"Meaning, I don't think you've been entirely honest and open with me," I said, trying not to sound like a petulant asshole. "I mean, when were you going to tell me— about the trans thing?"

"Did *she?*" Zip's face, which up till this morning had pretty much always been genial and kind, darkened to a shade of purple-gray. He clenched his napkin in his fist. "Oohh, that *girl*…"

"It's not anything to be ashamed of," Sonya said, this time putting a gentle hand on his fist. "Remember: no shame. Don't apologize."

"I'm not ashamed," Zip growled, sounding like Clint Eastwood in a very bad mood. "I just don't want my business being *broadcast* all over the place. Geez. It's the disrespect; the behind-the-back thing that gets me."

"So, it's true," I said, trying to get back on track.

"Yeah, of course it's true. I was raised as a girl till I was about three, and my parents said shortly after I started to string sentences together, I started expressing my thoughts, as in 'I boy.' I hated wearing the ruffly, girly outfits they'd try to put me in. And I was *such* a jock." He laughed, and the happy Zip, I'd become used to, reappeared. "My poor parents. After two older boys who were the usual Jewish-intellectual types, and another daughter, they *finally* get a star athlete. Man, I killed at Pee-Wee football, hockey, the whole works."

"But…" I floundered. "But you're—"

"Yeah, I'm on hormone blockers, so at least that took care of some things. But I can't have breast surgery until I'm eighteen. Beyond that…" He shrugged. "I just take it day by day."

"Have you gotten any flack in the locker room?" I asked. I was, admittedly, curious.

"No, most kids don't know the whole story, I don't think. Maybe an occasional rumor. I came into Jefferson in ninth grade, and I've always presented myself as male, because that's who I am; that's how I identify. So it's never really been an issue, except when the stupid office people make a mistake sometimes, because I have to list my full legal name with the school, until I change it."

"Will you keep it as Zip?" I asked, intrigued.

"Sure, why not? That's what people call me," he grinned. "Would you ever legally change yours to Shan?"

He had me there. "Probably not. It's my grandfather's name," I sighed.

"But you get tired of having to explain yourself," Zip added.

"I do, but it's actually just me explaining my name, not *myself*."

"'Never complain, never explain,'" Sonya put in.

"Oooh, I like that. Did you make that up?"

"No," Sonya said. "Prime Minister Benjamin Disraeli said it, but Greta Garbo popularized it in an old movie."

"Who's Greta Garbo?" I asked.

"Oh honey," Sonya sighed sadly. "You're a sweetheart, but you are culturally illiterate. Next thing, you'll tell us you've never seen *Harold and Maude*."

Apparently, this was a very bad thing, but I had to admit, "What's that?"

Sonya and Zip gave each other significant looks. "Well, that's one for the future calendar," Sonya said, "if we can ever get a night with you away from swim practice and Kallie. Now, back to the subject…"

"Look," I said, holding up my hand; they were still looking at me as if I were something in a fishbowl. "I think I know where you're going. I was kind of worked up last night from the pressure of the whole evening, and… I appreciate what you're saying, but I probably just over-reacted."

"Dude, lots of people's first times suck," Zip said. "It's not that big a deal."

"When most guys overreact," Sonya said, "they hit a wall, or go drive a car somewhere fast, or do martial arts. Or play videogames, so they can blow a bunch of things up, or kill monsters."

"I do all those things," Zip said, helpfully. I blinked; Zip was probably in an unusual place, being as he'd seen life from both sides of the gender fence. And he was probably a lot more of a violent gamer than I was. We could never afford an X-box or Wii.

"*Anyways.*" Sonya seemed to be reaching the end of her tether. "Most guys don't burst into tears and go to the place you went last night, unless they really had a reason to."

"You've already said I'm not like other guys," I answered — craftily, if I say so myself. "I just need to do a better job managing my time and responsibilities and my emotions, so I don't get overwhelmed again. It's just— a lot of pressure to live up to."

"Well," Sonya said, slumping a little. I felt somewhat bad, as if I'd let her down somehow, but I needed her to understand what Kallie and the people she knew could do for me, for my mom. But I couldn't say that out loud to her and Zip. *"You're both nice, but I need to follow the A-listers to succeed at Jefferson, and that's not you."*

"We just want you to know," Zip said, finally scraping the last of the cheese from the plate, "that we want to be your friends, and we're around anytime you need us. But you'll have to *tell* us when that is, so we don't… overstep."

"Why would you think you're overstepping?" I asked, a little stiffly.

"Look at us," Zip said, gesturing to himself and Sonya. "Look at you. People make snap judgments in life. People stereotype, and read into things. And like it or not, people project stuff onto others."

"What are you projecting onto me?" I asked, my voice coming out a little rougher than I expected. "I don't need saving. Just because I'm nice doesn't mean I'm a pussy."

Zip and Sonya exchanged glances again. "We know," Zip said gently. "You never would've gotten this far in life if you couldn't take care of yourself. But we just wanted to remind you: you don't have to carry everything all alone on your back."

"If you start singing 'Lean On Me,'" Sonya said, gathering her purse and elbowing Zip out of the booth, "I will make you regret it."

"So, did we accomplish whatever we were going to accomplish here?" I asked, fishing for some change to leave my mom as a tip. Circle Of Life.

"Kind of," Sonya said, dropping a couple bills with my change. "Please thank you mom for us for breakfast."

"Yeah!" Zip said, grinning. "I'm going to have to come here more often!"

As we left, waving goodbye to my mom as we went out, I felt a slight pang. It was a great breakfast. I just didn't know when — or how — I'd be able to do it again, if Kallie ever found out about it.

Which did give me pause, again: was I *afraid* of the girl who was supposed to be my girlfriend?

Chapter 12

After all that, Kallie wasn't in school that day.

But it seemed like she was.

As I was walking into school, my phone buzzed. I momentarily thought it was my mom, telling me I'd left something at the coffee shop, but it wasn't.

KILLER HEADACHE 2DAY STAYING HOME. CAN U GET MY HW & COME BY L8ER? YER A DOLL. XXOOO K.

The weird thing was, even though I'd suggested having breakfast away from campus, and even though Kallie wasn't there, I felt like everyone she knew was watching me. Her friend Sierra — the preppy chick with the shiny lip gloss — stopped me in the commons and asked me if I'd gotten Kallie's text. I was too bewildered to ask why *she* wasn't bringing Kallie her homework. People from her lunch table on Monday seemed to be scrutinizing me extra-carefully when I passed them in the halls. I wondered if she'd told a friend about last night, and rumors had spread.

By the time I hit swim practice, I definitely had the Lil Jon/LMFAO song 'Outta Your Mind' ricocheting around in my skull like a hostile pinball. *"Get outta your mind! Get outta your mind!"*

I gave practice everything I had, since our first meet was tomorrow night against Hardwicke Prep. My relay went well, but my hundred-meter freestyle lagged a bit from the other day. Both coaches seemed happy with me, but Coach Tsai just shrugged a little and said, "Good job, Shan. Not every time is going to be like the first."

He was trying to be nice, but it actually made me more frustrated, and I kind of grunted a response. He looked a little confused, but didn't push further.

It was odd, I realized: when I swam in the relay, I put all of my focus on just getting to the other person, and that gave me the impetus and drive to speed through the water. When it was just me against others, however, without someone actually depending on me, I had an attack of nerves and my stomach got queasy. Instead of focusing on how I was part of the team, an essential link in a chain, I started thinking about myself as a solo competitor trying to 'measure up.' Maybe it was the bathroom freak-out I'd had at Kallie's, but I was suddenly very hyper-aware of how much of a fraud I felt like in this environment, on this team.

I was in the shower thinking about all this, staring blankly at the tiled wall with rivulets of warm water running down my face, when I felt someone touch my shoulder and say "Hey." I turned, and who should be there but Theo, smiling gently, towel over his shoulder but also quite naked.

No, this wasn't weird at all.

"You're gonna do great this weekend," Theo said, as if he could read my mind. "Don't get too psyched out. If you swim like you did on Monday, you're going to blow everyone out of the water." He grinned even bigger. *"Literally."*

I actually grinned myself. "Isn't it funny how these days everyone uses the word literally in situations where it *literally* makes no sense?"

"But in our case it does," Theo said. "Because, pool. Water."

"Yeah, got it," I said.

"Hey, if you ever want to practice," he said, "work on some techniques, I have a pool. You can come over some weekend, if you wanted to hang out. We could practice some strokes, maybe watch a movie."

I was completely flummoxed by how to respond to this (especially the phrase "practice some *strokes*"), but my first instinct told me I'd better get out of the shower and dressed. "Yeah…maybe sometime. Well— see ya." I turned off the water and beat a retreat out of the shower area, trying not to walk too fast, lest he notice.

Several aisles away out of sight, standing in front of my locker, my mind started racing again. Did Theo know I knew about him? Did he know I knew about him and Eddie? Was he making a pass at me? Or was he just trying to get information about my date with Kallie?

I jerked my underwear and pants on, fumbling in my haste. I hadn't done a towel-off in the shower per usual, so now my hair was dripping all over my gym bag and clothes. I grabbed my stuff and crammed it into the bag, ducked by the mirror and swiped a wad of paper towels quickly over my hair.

In the far distance behind me, I saw Theo walking to his locker. Another kid hooted at him, and another guy snapped his towel at Theo's ass, but he just kept walking and didn't break stride.

I could never be that cool.

Biking to Kallie's wasn't terribly far — as she'd said, she lived only ten minutes from school, just in the opposite direction of my house. However, I'd been so involved yesterday watching her hair blow in the wind and anticipating dinner, I hadn't really noticed that the last mile or two of the trip was largely uphill. In a convertible BMW, it was a great drive.

Today, by the time I made it to the big driveway in front of the house, around five thirty, all of the cool, refreshing feeling I'd had from swim practice and my shower were gone, and that, combined with nerves, now had me a sweaty mess. I could only imagine what Parsons thought when he saw me, but his face was the picture of composure as he descended the front steps and nodded hello.

"Miss Kallie is down at the pool," he said, each syllable perfectly enunciated like Henry Higgins in *My*

Fair Lady, one of my mom's favorite movies. "She requested that you bring her homework down to her there. If you would like to take a swim, I've taken the liberty of laying out swimming clothes for you."

They had spare swimsuits for teenage boys? Oh, right: Eddie. I swallowed as Parsons walked around through the side gate, gesturing for me to follow him. I didn't know what to do with my bike, so I just put down the kickstand and left it by the front porch, and followed him in.

The side of the house was all manicured gardens and hedges. When we reached the back, we crossed a lawn and looked down. Below several tiers of more hedges and flowers was the pool, with a little cottage next to it — changing rooms, I supposed. Kallie was reclining in a chaise longue, basking in the late-afternoon sun, wearing a cerulean-blue bikini bottom and a pair of sunglasses. What she wasn't wearing was a bikini top.

Parsons didn't seem to notice, or had willed himself not to. He gestured to the staircase, and I slowly descended, him calling out behind me, "Please telephone the house if you would like a beverage." You knew it was something special the way he said "bever*age*," as in rhyming with *garage*, as opposed to just "a drink."

I was just wondering what I was going to say as a greeting when she heard my footsteps approaching and turned her head. "Oh, *there* you are," she said, and I couldn't tell if that meant "Oh, I'm glad to see you" versus "Where the hell have you been?"

"Here I am," I said, setting my backpack down and taking a seat on the edge of the chair. I was wondering what the appropriate greeting etiquette was for a moment like this, but Kallie just scooted forward, put her arms around me and kissed me, bikini top or no. I had to say, it felt amazing, as if I hadn't realized how addicted I was to her touch.

I ran my hands down her back, feeling the warmth of her skin, letting the kiss build before I finally broke away.

"I brought you your stuff," I said.

"I knew you would," she smiled. "You're an angel."

"Did you really have a headache?" I didn't know why I asked that, or why it was suddenly very important that I knew the answer.

"I did this morning," she said, looking me right in the eyes, as though she knew what I was thinking. "But after lunch it got a lot better. But I figured, why drive into school for two classes? Besides, *Kill Bill* was on HBO."

"Your mom didn't care?" I asked, mystified. My mom was a Nazi about my education, probably due to the half a year I'd missed while we were hiding. Unless I had a fever of over a hundred and one, or was puking blood, she made sure I was going to school.

"My mom is in Seattle for the day," she smirked. "Part of her women's club thingy. And my dad is meeting her for dinner. They won't be home until ten at the earliest."

"So…" My mind was simultaneously turned on and terrified of what that might mean.

"So," she said, standing up and taking my hand, pulling me to the changing cabin before I had time to think or speak. It wasn't much more than a cabana, but it did have a main room with a TV, a large couch, a little kitchenette with a microwave and sink, and a little bathroom and shower. I absorbed all of this in about two and a half seconds as she pushed the door shut behind us.

This time was different, maybe because all she needed to do was untie the strings on the sides of her bikini, and she already had the home court advantage. Yesterday, I realized, she'd taken her time with me, getting me comfortable bit by bit, act by act, until I was too far gone to resist.

Today, because I wasn't wearing formal clothes, she had my shirt off and discarded in seconds, and everything else followed moments later. Then we were on the couch, me on top this time, and things proceeded apace.

There were no handcuffs or anything else, thankfully. She still used her fingernails a lot; I could feel them digging into my back, scraping over my muscles, hopefully not leaving marks. And since the house was a significant distance away, we didn't even have to be as discrete about noise as we'd been in her room, which was good.

When we were finished, the light coming through the blinds was extra-blinding, and the room was hot. It was that hour before sunset when everything gets super-intense. Kallie stretched, wiped her damp hair back from her forehead. "Whew. Studmuffin."

I couldn't help it: I glowed a little. Today, I felt strong, and masculine, and desirable: everything I hadn't felt yesterday. She couldn't have inflated my ego more if she'd consciously tried. (Was she trying?)

She ran one finger down my chest, around my nipple. "Ready for a cool-off dip?"

"Sure," I said, propping myself up on one elbow. I was an even sweatier, stickier mess than when I'd first arrived at the house. "Parsons said something about a swimsuit…"

"Oh puh-*leaze*," she said dismissively, getting to her feet and extending a hand to me. "No one's around. Come on, the water feels great when you're naked."

I hedged. I'd skinny-dipped on hikes before, but that was out in the woods far away from everyone. Still, Parsons was safely up at the house, and Kallie's mom and dad weren't due back for a couple hours…

The wild beast she'd awakened in me growled, and came to life. "All right, let's go for it."

Coming back outside into the baking sun made us screech like vampires, and the pavement was searing on our bare feet. She grabbed my hand and pulled me as we sort-of jumped/fell into the deep end, which was only about eight feet, sinking to the bottom, then erupting like geysers from the surface.

I shook the water and hair out of my eyes, laughing, looked at her smiling at me, all kitty-cat smugness. All of the anxiety and weirdness I'd been feeling for the past twenty-four hours was in abeyance, and I felt on top of the world. Why had I been such a head case? So I had a girlfriend who was a freak in the bedroom; what was to complain about? Most guys would've killed to have someone who was as sexually voracious as Kallie.

Thinking about it, I pulled her to me and kissed her again, as she wrapped her legs around my waist. I paddle-pushed us over to the edge of the pool, pressed her up against the wall, kissing her some more as she positioned our bodies, and—

"*Jesus,* Kallie — get a fucking room, would you?"

"You should talk," Kallie yelled, breaking off the kiss.

I turned. The evening sun was in my eyes, and the figure was largely in silhouette, standing by the pool looking down at us. Not earlier with Theo, not more recently with Kallie in the changing cabin, not *ever* that I could recollect had I been so aware of my nakedness as I was now.

Eddie.

He looked like the picture on Kallie's bulletin board, but that must have been a year or two ago, and apparently he'd spent every minute since then at the gym. His neck was thick, and his arms and chest looked almost inflated; his back was broad enough to project a movie on. He wore a tight tank top that emphasized his Hulk-like upper body, threatening to turn it into shreds of fabric at any moment; his thighs were like ham hocks, and his calves like baseballs. His hair was close-cropped, and his black Irish features glowered in the sun.

"You know you're not supposed to mess around in the pool," he yelled back. "Who's this?"

"This is Shan," Kallie said, very deliberately running her hands over my lower backside and butt, grabbing it, pulling me into her, almost as if she were taunting her brother. "Shan, Eddie."

"Hey," I said, weakly. All of my bravado from a few short minutes ago had vanished, along with my clothing, my self-respect, and my erection.

"Shan," Eddie said, as though it was a word that tasted unfamiliar in his mouth. "Like Shannon? Isn't that a girl's name?"

"Wasn't Eddie one of the Munsters?" Kallie shot back, open contempt in her voice. (Had she read my mind on the Addams family comparison?) "And why are you here? Mom and Dad are in town, so there's no one to ask for money."

"I don't need money," Eddie said, walking (oh God) around the pool towards us. "I have lots right now.

I've been working at the gym and the supplement store, besides enrolling at North Seattle. So get off my ass."

A gym rat *and* taking supplements; no wonder he was starting to resemble the Michelin tire guy.

"Then why are you here?" Kallie almost snarled. The edge I'd seen flashes of this past week was suddenly there and gleaming, ready to strike. I pulled away from her and paddled off a bit, turning at an angle so I wasn't flashing Eddie my junk.

"I want my gun," Eddie said. My heart and stomach both lurched.

"Too bad, Dad has all of them in the safe."

"I *want* it!" Eddie turned even darker with rage.

"Well, you can come by tomorrow when he's here, or call him and ask for the combination," Kallie said, reaching up and pulling a towel off the edge of the pool to wrap around herself. I, however, was still left naked in the water. "You're the big boy going to *community college*. Figure it out by yourself."

"You're a bitch," Eddie spat, turning and stomping away.

"You're an asshole," Kallie rejoined, "and if you keep shooting up steroids your balls are going to wither up and fall off!"

Eddie flipped her off as he climbed the stairs, looking like some sort of mutant on its way back to its lair. I noticed as the sun hit his back that he did have a lot of back acne; a sure sign, as Kallie said, of someone abusing steroids.

Kallie sloshed her way out of the pool, towel wrapped around her, everything about her seething. "God, he is *such* a dick. Sorry about that. Oh," she suddenly realized, "you need a towel. Here." She grabbed an extra one and tossed it to me. It fell in the pool and was immediately soaked, but I didn't care. I just wanted something wrapped around me at that moment.

"I guess," I said, a little meaningfully, "I should've worn a swimsuit."

"Oh, whatever," she said, striding out of the water, towel clinging damply to her body. "Don't worry about him. He's just throwing his weight around, trying to make up for the fact that he graduated two years ago, and is barely doing anything with his life." She grabbed another towel and furiously dried her hair, as I slowly ambled towards the pool stairs, wondering if there was another dry towel somewhere I could use.

"So, he doesn't live here?"

"He shares a house with some loser friends," Kallie said, wrapping the towel around her head, turban-style. "All they do all day is lift and obsess over their bodies. That thing with Theo really messed him up. He's convinced it was because Theo didn't find him attractive enough." She snorted. "Gorilla."

"How long did they date?" I asked, trying to sound casual. I was interested in any insight I might glean into not only Eddie's head, but also Theo's.

"Just two, three months. Theo broke it off when he heard about the rumor." Kallie gathered her things, looking at me as if I were holding us up. I was still standing there in a sopping wet towel.

"What rumor?" I asked, innocently.

"Oh, you know," she said acidly, looking at me as if I were stupid for trying to play her. "Everyone knows. Please. He hasn't touched peanut butter since, lest someone sees him and it starts all over again."

"So…"

"All evidence must be suppressed," she said, meaningfully. "In case you didn't notice, we don't have a dog running around here any more. She's gone."

"Gone?" *As in given away, or shot?*

"Why don't you go get dressed," she said, ignoring my hanging question and moving to the stairs. "There should be one more towel hanging in the cottage bathroom. Put on your clothes, and come up to the house. We'll have some dinner, maybe watch a movie before you have to go home." She was climbing up towards the lawn before I even made a move towards the cabin.

A little while later, we were standing in the palatial kitchen, making pizzas. Kallie had put on some sort of designer blouse and shorts, and I was still in my clothes from school. Parsons must have anticipated our hunger, or maybe Kallie spoke with him while I was dressing, as there were balls of dough laid out for us on a platter by the stove, along with a jar of tomato sauce, a bowl of shredded cheese, and various ramekins with mushrooms, olives, diced jalapeno peppers, pineapple, and the like.

"Oooh, japaleno!" Kallie squealed. "I love these things. Here, try one."

"No thanks," I said, my fingers full of mushrooms and olives. As I've said, I don't like peppers. I mean, I *really* don't like them.

"Come *on*," she said, waving a jalapeno at me. Her eyes were flashing mischief. Had I had more of my radar up, I would've remembered seeing that look the other night in her bedroom, the look that said, *Don't even try to say no.*

"I don't like jalapenos," I said, moving my arm to block her. In a flash, she had her fingers in my ribs, tickling me and poking me with her fingers, while the other hand waved the chunk of green, seeded vegetation dangerously close to my eyes.

I doubled over, crying "Stop!" and she took advantage of my defenselessness to stuff a jalapeno in my mouth. My stomach heaved. Without even thinking about it, I turned and promptly puked into the sink. Well, mostly in the sink.

"Jesus!" Kallie screamed. It was a terrible sound, high and raw with rage. I'd spewed some of my vomit on her accidentally, and it was now dripping down her shirt, my lunch and morning breakfast of biscuits et al., mingled with bile and other nastiness. The smell was

horrendous, but I could barely focus on it through the barrage of invective now being hurled at me. "You stupid, *fucking idiot!*"

The slap came at my shoulders, then my arms; then she was using both hands, apoplectic with rage, raining punches and slaps down on me. As I ducked my head, her hand caught me across the face, landing a stinging slap on my jaw. My face, as well as my stomach, was now burning, and tears came to my eyes.

She paused long enough in the assault, wild-eyed, to stare at me with incredulity, as if I were something completely incomprehensible to her, something that she didn't know how to handle, besides beating it into submission. When she spoke, her voice was trying to be steady, but it was still shaking with fury. "Do you have any idea, Mr Swimming *Scholarship*, how much this shirt cost?"

"I can't eat jalapenos," I said weakly, tears still running down my face. I had no idea if it was a side effect from vomiting, a reaction to the stench of the pepper right under my nose, or pain from the torrent of blows she'd inflicted upon me. "You shouldn't... have— I'm sorry."

"You're sorry." The words sounded like a dead foreign language, the way she let them fall off her tongue. "You're *sorry*. This is a Michael Kors top I got on *sale* for six hundred dollars. What is *wrong* with you? Normal people don't have a reaction to food like that!"

"Maybe it's an allergy," I said weakly, running my arm quickly across my eyes. "I don't know. I've always reacted like that to them. I really am sorry."

"Go rinse your mouth," she spat, shoving me as if the sight of me made her physically ill. "Go use the bathroom. I'll get the kitchen cleaned up. *Parsons!*" She yelled with every bit of force she seemed to have in her body. The old man appeared, not quite running but certainly walking with a lot more speed than he seemed used to.

"Clean this up," Kallie commanded, her voice like a razor blade. "Throw it away. Throw it all away. I don't want to eat it if he threw up on any part of it."

"Yes, Miss Kallie," Parsons said tremulously, as I left the kitchen, watching the sad little pizzas we'd made swept off the counter into the trash. Kallie stormed past him and headed upstairs, presumably to change her top. I could hear her feet stomping furiously all the way up.

I sat in the same bathroom I'd been in the other night, when I'd had the panic attack at dinner; same little soaps, same seashell motif. I looked at myself in the mirror, which was not a real good decision at that moment. I was flushed with sunburn from earlier that afternoon (that's what I got for not remembering sunscreen) and I had a film around the edge of my mouth. I rinsed that off first. I also had a cut near my temple from something; either Kallie's nails, or maybe one of the rings she was wearing. I put a little soap and water on it. It didn't look terrible yet, but it stung like hell.

My stomach felt sour and squeezed-out, the way it does after you empty it. I knew later I'd be starving beyond belief, but I really didn't want to ask Kallie about any other food, in case she went off on one again. I didn't know much about fashion, but apparently Michael Kors was a pretty big name in designers, and I'd really messed up by yakking on her. For some reason, I was so mortified and embarrassed that I'd ruined her top — and that it would take me months to even hope of paying her back or buying another one — that I didn't even focus on her going off on me in the kitchen.

Why did I shrink and cower under these sorts of circumstances? Why did I seem incapable of moving, or standing up for myself?

I rinsed out my mouth and exited the bathroom, and ran right smack into Eddie in the hallway. He looked even bigger up close, and I felt an involuntary shudder run through me.

"She still upstairs?" he said, almost in a friendly manner.

"Yeah," I said. "I— we had an accident in the kitchen. She's changing."

"Into what, a human being?" he snorted. "The She-Devil herself? Not likely."

I didn't know what to say. I felt like I should defend her. Eddie had done nothing so far to endear himself to me, but I once again found myself rooted in place and tongue-tied. I was also unsure what I should or shouldn't talk about. Mentioning Theo would be a surefire trigger for something scary, and I had no idea if Eddie had succeed in his quest to obtain his gun. Guns. This had very strong possibilities of not ending well.

"Listen," he said, leaning forward, suddenly conspiratorial. "I know you know things about me. People talk. She talks. The school's small."

I felt like I was on an icy pond, and spider cracks were beginning to run in all directions from right under my feet. I played it as noncommittal as possible: "Yeah."

"So, you heard. The peanut butter story." He didn't look ashamed or anything, just expectant, as if awaiting confirmation. I nodded, slowly and cautiously.

"Yeah. That's been going around for a while now." He leaned in closer to me, and I involuntarily pressed my back against the wall next to the bathroom. He actually smelled kind of nice due to an abundance of cologne, but his eyes kept darting back and forth, as if they were searchlights scanning my face, and his overwhelming bulk was pretty intimidating. He leaned one huge paw up above my head, bent in close, and lowered his voice to a scratchy whisper. "What no one knows is, *she's* the one who started that rumor."

I think that whatever air that was in my lungs turned into liquid nitrogen. I would've gasped, but you can't gasp frozen crystals, can you?

Eddie slowly smirked, even as his face darkened. "Don't ever turn on her or cross her: she'll do things you can't even imagine. Yeah. She'll even shoot your puppy, and then wipe her prints off the gun, so she could claim that I did it because *I* was so ashamed and disturbed. Me, the guy who took care of that puppy since it was just a few weeks old." A quick spasm of pain crossed his features, and I saw a lonely teenage boy who loved his little puppy. Until.

"So," he went on, snapping back into himself. "My advice to you. Keep saying *yes.* Don't piss her off. And— do you talk to Theo?"

Oh, now I was really starring in the Night Of The Long Knives.

"Yeah, you do. I can see it on your face. Listen. Tell him I'm sorry, okay? I didn't— just tell him that. My whole family went after him, but her most of all. I seriously thought she might kill him, for ruining our perfect little model of a perfect family." A door slammed upstairs, and the urgency of his speech increased. "You've got to know you've been cast, my friend — cast as the perfect, pretty, caring boyfriend to perfect, pretty Kallie Corcoran. You better learn your lines and hit your marks, because you *do not* want to be replaced in her script. She'll never let you go without a lot of bad, bad drama going down first."

He pulled away, and patted his coat jacket pocket meaningfully. I suddenly realized he must have had something, some sort of handgun, in there the entire time. But he just murmured, "For protection," and I had a weird flash of insight: maybe he wasn't looking for his gun to start trouble. Maybe he was looking for a way to keep himself safe from trouble, depending on how bad it got.

He exited the front door just as his sister hit the bottom of the stairs. They passed each other without speaking, tension boiling in the air between them like a summer thunderstorm. Kallie approached me, still standing in the hallway; she'd changed her top into something else that looked nice, but darned if I knew anything about it. As I said, I'm not up on designers or brands.

Her mouth was a little line and her eyes were still flashing. She crossed her arms, waiting for me to speak first. After a pause, I did. "I told you I was sorry."

"So you said," she replied flatly. "Actions speak louder than words. But I forgive you."

I was so relieved that she wasn't angry any more — well, not as angry as she had been — that it didn't occur to me to ask her to apologize for slapping me. She went on, "But you can make it up to me."

"How?"

"I'll let you stay and watch a movie with me," she said, suddenly magnanimous. "It's still early."

It was actually seven thirty, and I did some quick math in my head. If a movie ran at least ninety minutes, and I biked home afterwards, I wasn't going to get home until after ten, and I hadn't even touched my homework.

I mentally riffed through my classes: I could finish reading my short story and do the Language Arts assignment when I got home, my science lab was a group thing not due until Monday, and I'd text Sonya and ask her to help me with math, or just let me copy her answers, before school tomorrow. Spanish, we were just doing translations in the Language Lab, and that left history. Fortunately, my history teacher, Mr Franks, was the kind of guy who seemed to be letting a pile of work accumulate in the "turn-in" basket, and then he'd take everything home and marathon-grade over the weekend. Since I already had two assignments turned in, that would buy me time until Monday.

As I hesitated, I saw her face darken. "If it's too much *trouble* for you to hang out with me—"

"No, it's fine," I interrupted quickly, lest her mood begin to sour again. "I can do a movie."

"Great," she said, turning and pulling my arm with her towards the TV room with the giant sofas. My stomach growled, and I hoped she couldn't hear it; the last thing I was going to do was ask for food, even though a bowl of popcorn would've been nice while watching TV. The mini pizzas were long gone.

She opened a cabinet filled with DVDs. "We've got all this stuff, and we also have On-Demand, so several hundred choices. What do you like?"

"I like comedies," I said truthfully. When I was a kid and we had even less money than we do now, my mom would check out old Marx Brothers and Laurel and Hardy comedies from the library to watch on our ancient VCR, and we would watch them together and laugh and laugh. She also let me see things kids my age weren't supposed to see because she thought they were important, like *Blazing Saddles* and *The Birdcage*. "As long as you can laugh," she said, "the bastards never win."

"Oh, comedies are stupid," Kallie said dismissively. "They never make really funny movies I. I like watching horror movies, and laughing at them."

"Why would you laugh at a horror movie?" I asked.

"Because they're so stupid," she said. "The *people* in them are stupid. Like, in *The Strangers* or *Funny Games*, or *Saw*. They're just dumb. It's a relief when they get killed."

My stomach gurgled again; from hunger, nausea, or nerves, I couldn't any more.

"Here," she said, pulling *Hostel* from the shelf. "This is good. It's from Eli Roth, who did the *Saw* movies."

"I thought you wanted to watch a comedy," I said. The picture on the DVD case looked disturbing.

"I asked you what you liked, and *you* said comedy," she said, as if explaining it to a three-year-old. "This is really funny, watch."

It was only ninety-three minutes, so I acquiesced, despite a feeling of foreboding. It was a pretty standard-issue horror movie, with an emphasis on lots of gore. Not a lot of fun for a guy with a still-sour gut. Kallie laughed when one guy got his Achilles tendon sliced, and tried to crawl away. "Look, he's such a tool!"

"He's hurt," I said, trying not to sound irritable. She'd curled up next to me, and very forthrightly took my arm and wrapped it around her. Some people supposedly find scary horror movies to be a turn-on; the violence in this didn't turn me on, it just turned my stomach.

"Oh please," she said. "Look, he's going to die now."

I shut my eyes. It's not like she was looking at me, anyways. I didn't like listening to all the screaming and people begging for their lives, but at least I didn't have to watch it. Since her head was on my chest, she had to physically turn it to see my face, so I could always open my eyes right before she saw they were closed.

When the movie ended, I didn't know what to say. Thanks for the great sex earlier? Or, gee, this dinner and a movie thing sure sucked? By now, I was starving.

"I guess you have to go," she said, sighing resignedly as she turned the TV off. "My parents won't be home till late, we could actually hide your bike and you could stay over. I'd sneak you out in the morning."

"I'd better get home and finish my homework," I said honestly. "And don't you have to do the work I brought you?"

"Oh, that," she said dismissively. "I might. I could've done it tomorrow. I just wanted to see you."

I was stunned. "You had me bike all the way up here, and bring me your homework just because you wanted me to come *see* you?"

"I get scared when I'm in the house alone," she mock-pouted as we were walking to the door. I eyed a mounted sword. "Dangerous people everywhere. Didn't the movie teach you anything? And what's wrong with a girl wanting to see her boyfriend?"

"Are we officially boyfriend and girlfriend?" I asked, confusedly. Despite all of the high-pressure going on from Kallie's family, I couldn't remember actually having had a moment where I'd said, "Yes, this is official now."

"Well, as they say at weddings: 'Speak now, or forever hold your peace,'" she said, playfully but with an undertone that was deadly serious. "Want to speak, or hold?"

And I thought about it, for a few very long seconds. I thought about the pool house, and how good it was. And I thought about the kitchen, and how bad that was. And how weird this house made me feel. And how right now I was completely starving, but didn't want to ask for food in case it triggered Kallie going off on me.

And I thought of my mom's face, and saw her sitting in the front row at the pool while they put a medal around my neck, crying tears of happiness, for once.

Kallie smiled, put her hands on both sides of my face, leaned in, and kissed me, offering a secure little smile. "That's what I thought."

It was a long bike ride home.

Chapter 13

When I woke up the next morning, I felt as though I'd spent the night sleeping on a bunch of rocks. I glared through one eye at the morning sun streaming into my room, pushed back the covers, and swiveled my body out of bed, feeling the muscles in my back and sides contract and stretch with reluctance. I pulled down the boxer shorts that had wedged their way up my thighs and turned into some sort of loincloth, and cast a look at the mirror hanging on my open closet door.

Oh, Jesus.

As part of ninth-grade health class, we'd studied the AIDS virus and symptoms of the condition. I remembered being freaked out by photos of patients who were covered with dark, purple blotches called Karposi's Sarcoma, a skin condition many people with AIDS used to contract before there were medicines to help manage the disease.

And now, there, all up and down my torso, were bruises: at least four of them that I could see. One on my chest was dark purple, one near my shoulder was sort of purply-yellow, another on the back of my shoulder was a hot peppery pink, and another down near my ribs was an angry-looking red with bits of purple smeared through it. For all I knew, I might have had another one on my back; I couldn't turn far enough around to see it.

But I suddenly realized why I'd only opened one eye, and why I was having a hard time with depth perception: my right eye — the one that had had a cut next to it last night — was now swollen, and only opened about halfway. I'd cleaned out the cut, but it looked like some blood vessels had broken under the skin, and the whole area around my eye was discolored and weird-looking.

This was not good. This was not good. This was *not good.*

Last night, my mom had been in bed when I'd come in. Since I'd called her just after leaving Kallie's, she knew I was on my way home, so I didn't have to say much more than, "Hi, I'm home safe, very tired, good night" and duck into my room, staying up until eleven finishing my English assignment. Sonya, thankfully, was a night owl (the other night at school had proven that), and was still up when I'd texted her to ask about meeting before school to discuss math; of course, she'd said yes.

The problem was, my mom wasn't working this morning, and I needed to get out of the house without her asking questions. My brain was racing like a hamster on speed, ready to blast one of those little running wheels into hyperspace: what to do what to do *whattodowhattodowhattodowhattodo?*

I looked at the clock: six forty-five. If I took the world's fastest shower, maybe I could get out of the house before seven, as my mom liked to wake up by watching the TV morning shows and having coffee during her mornings off.

I grabbed clean underwear and poked my head out; all quiet. I ducked into the bathroom, closing the door quietly behind me, and opened the window a crack rather than turning on the fan. In the bathroom light, without the diffusion of my curtains and dark blue walls, the bruises looked even more pronounced, especially since I hadn't been out in the sun the past few weeks and my torso was on the paler side. When I ran the soap over the colored patches on my body, the muscles and skin shrieked with pain. I'd need to borrow an ice pack when I got to school to try to get the eye down; I needed to see during our first swim meet Saturday.

Swimming. I stared in shock at the tile wall of the shower, letting the water run down my face and over my pulsing eye. What was I going to say about this at swimming practice? There was no way to cover up these bruises with waterproof makeup, even if I knew anything about how to use it, which I didn't.

I turned off the water, grabbed my towel (never thought I'd be glad to see my own towel), did a quick dry-off, and went to work on brushing my teeth. I was lucky I hadn't bitten my lip; all of my gums were intact, too. Phew.

I skedaddled back to my room and grabbed clothes; I'd tried to look a little nice this week, trying to stay within Jefferson's dress code (no blue jeans or T-shirts) but also making an effort to "class up" with polo shirts and the like. Today, I just grabbed the first buttoned shirt with long sleeves and a high collar I could lay my hands on, along with a pair of black jeans my mom had magically found at Value Village. Homework, keys, swim bag was at school. Boom. On our way.

I was just heading towards the front door when I heard the TV click on; oh no. Sure enough, as the screen came into focus and the news anchor began blathering the headlines, my mom came around the corner in her robe, coffee in hand. "Are you going to dash off without saying goodbye?"

"Good morning, good-bye," I said, kissing her cheek from my left side, so that she saw my unmarked temple. Too late, she grabbed my shoulder and gasped. "What *happened*?"

"Bike accident," I said, so easily and so naturally, I surprised myself. Of course, what else? "I hit something in the road and took a tumble. I'm fine, really."

"Oh honey," my mom said, sounding like I'd just broken her heart into a thousand pieces, as if I were joining Hitler Youth or something. "Don't you have a light on your bike?"

Thinking fast: "Yes, but the battery's dead."

"Shannon!" Oh crud, now she was mad; her face ignited with irritation. "How many times do I have to

tell you to take *care* of yourself? I'm not going to be here forever, you know. I can't be responsible for you all the time! You've got to start thinking about the future."

I am, Mom, I am. "I know, I'm sorry." All I seemed to do lately was apologize.

"Oh, go to school," she said, almost shoving me to the door, shaking her head in exasperation. I knew she wasn't really mad, but I still felt like crap for lying, and for making her think I was disappointing her.

Well, this day was certainly off to a grand start.

"What happened to you?" Sonya said, her voice rising almost as high as her eyebrows as I locked my bike.

"Bike accident last night."

"Mmmm," she said concernedly, taking my chin gently in her hand and turning my face side to side. "Poor baby. I'll show you where the nurse is and get you an ice pack."

"Thanks," I said. "You're awesome."

"I know," she said sweetly. "All right, let's get some ice, and then get on some geometry?"

"Sure. Is Zip meeting us?"

"Eventually," she said, her voice full of foreboding. I must've looked at her strangely, because she laughed. "He decided that as a payback from yesterday's sumptuous breakfast, he's swinging by the best bagelry he knows, and bringing us lox sandwiches. You like lox, right?"

"Love it." I did, too, even though I'd only had it a couple times, due to how expensive it is. I was momentarily envious of Zip, then really appreciative of him for being so nice.

We were in the nurse's office, getting me an ice pack when — speak of the devil — Zip showed up. There must have been something in the air, because his right leg had a streak of road rash down it that was Ing every color in a Grand Canyon sunset.

"Holy merde," Sonya almost-screeched as the nurse ran for antiseptic. "Are you okay?"

"Kind of," Zip said, gloomily. "But my bike isn't. The front tire's messed up really good."

"Oh my God," Sonya said, "I am never letting you two out of my sight again. Shan had an accident last night."

"No way," Zip said, looking at me with surprise. I dropped the ice pack from my eye, and he winced. "Ouch."

"I haven't even applied anything yet," the nurse said, bewildered, as she returned with alcohol swabs and bandages.

"No, him," Zip said, indicating my eye.

"Aye," I said, pointing at my eye as we both started giggling like idiots. We were becoming a Marx Brothers' routine.

Sonya wasn't in the mood for trifling. "Seriously, talk to me. What happened?"

"I was riding to school," Zip said sing-song, as if reciting a nursery rhyme, "because my parents were at the deli early this morning, and I needed to swing by there to get us breakfast. Oh, here!" His face lit up as he proffered a crumpled, torn bag that had still been clutched tightly in one hand this entire time. In it were two gorgeous, foil-wrapped bagel sandwiches, which Sonya and I fell on as if we were starving. (I very nearly was, by this point.) The nurse scrammed, lest we accidentally bit her hand off.

"Anyways, bagels… deli…" Sonya said, mouth full.

"Oh yeah. So I'm biking, and this car pulls up right behind me, and I swear, the driver intentionally grazed me. Like, bumped me from behind. So I fell over, and discovered the front wheel of my bike is now all bent, which made the ride that much more interesting. Thank *you*, mystery driver," he said, doing one of those fancy little actor-bows that you see sometimes at Shakespeare plays.

"You didn't see who it was?" Sonya said, suspiciously.

Zip shook his head. "I went down too fast, and it took me a minute to collect myself. And the food," he grinned sheepishly.

"Well, thank you for the treat," Sonya said.

"Yeah," I said. "This is amazing."

"Gotta fatten you two up," Zip said cheerfully, as we gathered our things. "It's my goal, by the end of the year, to be known as The Skinny One."

"Could happen," Sonya said doubtfully, handing me her math notebook. "Shan, why don't you and Zip grab a quiet table somewhere out of the way, so he can get my math homework down? I've got to take a trip to the ladies' room."

"Why out of the way?" Zip asked. "Are you ashamed to be seen with us?"

"Absolutely not," Sonya said, crisply. "However, I don't think Kallie Corcoran will take kindly to us not realizing that she is the center of the universe — or at least Shan's."

"She's not the center of my universe," I said, a little more defensively than I would've liked. "She's just my girlfriend."

"Oh-ho," Sonya said, meaningfully, as she strode off.

"Over here," Zip said, gesturing around a pillar. There was a little table in the corner behind the snack machines that had a direct view of the espresso cart, but no one ever sat there, preferring to take their morning snacks and beverages over in the main cluster of tables in the center of the commons.

I sat, gratefully, finishing the last bites of my sandwich, watching the morning light hit Zip's face and hair, creating an aura behind him. Not to be goopy, but he actually glowed.

"Good?" Zip said, breaking my thoughts.

"Yeah, you are," I said. I hadn't planned on it, I just said it. He was. He was a genuinely kind and good person.

Zip actually blushed. "Aww," he said, and then there was one of those nice awkward moments — the kind where neither person knows what to say, but you kind of smile at each other, and it's fine just the way it is.

I started copying Sonya's notes while Zip fiddled with his phone, looking for some good music. Finding a 70's funk station, he stuck one earbud in his ear and the other in mine. Parliament, "Give Up the Funk." Bliss.

In the far away distance, I saw Kallie come in, scanning the commons area and looking for me with a piqued expression, but then being greeted by one of her girlfriends. They chatted for a moment before Kallie disappeared into the office for first period.

Just as the bell rang, Sonya reappeared. "How's it going?"

"Great," I said, closing her notebook. It was, too. Her notes were perfect. Zip nodded happily.

"No problem," she said, taking it and sticking it in her bag. "I'll walk you to class."

"But don't you usually go the other way, with Zip?" I asked, confused.

"Yeah," Zip said. "I feel abandoned and neglected." He touched his heart like E.T. "Ouch."

"I'll catch up with you in a few," Sonya said, kissing her finger and applying it to Zip's cheek. He immediately perked up, waving at us as he went.

Sonya waited till Zip turned the corner, then took my arm. It wasn't mean, but it was firm and emphatic, and indicated she would not take *no* for an answer.

"What's up?" I asked, a sinking feeling taking my bagel sandwich to the bottom of my stomach.

"I put up with a lot here," Sonya said, eyes straight ahead, focused on something far away in the distance. She spoke very slowly and carefully. "Most people have no idea — *no* idea — what it's like being one of the only black kids in this school." She bit off the following words syllable by syllable: "It. Is. Ex-*haus*-ting."

"Uh-huh," I said, not quite following.

"I know some people say I have an attitude," she went on. "That's what people call it when you don't jump up and click your heels every time they go by. But sometimes, when your worst impressions or suspicions about people keep being confirmed, it gets really, *really* hard to keep up the happy front, day after day."

"Yeah…" I said, beginning to get a glimmer.

"And if you call people out on their crap," she said, her voice taking on a serrated tone, "all it does is get you labeled as difficult. The *Angry* girl."

"Are you mad at someone?" I asked, rhetorically.

Sonya stopped, pulled me aside next to the wall as the stream of teenagers drifted past us. Her eyes flashed.

"Yes. But the problem is, I'm not sure who I should be madder at — Kallie, or you."

"Me?" I felt a flash of panic, and the cold, damp prickles on my neck. "What did I do?"

"It's not what you did," Sonya said, acidly, "it's what you *didn't* do. Believe it or not, my favorite book series when I was a kid was Sherlock Holmes. He taught me some basic things about observing people and situations."

"Like…?"

"Like, for example," Sonya said, "the fact that you claim to have had a bike accident last night. However, I just checked your bike. No scratches. No bent spokes. Nothing to indicate you took a fall or had any sort of a problem — with your bike, at least."

The bagel in my stomach churned. "Sonya—"

"Zip, however," she went on, implacable and unstoppable as a tank, "*did* have a bike accident. And after I just went and checked your bike, I went and checked the cars in the parking lot. And I found a car that has a scratched-up, right front fender. The kind you might get if you intentionally tried to run someone off the road."

The bell rang. In the ensuing quiet, as the halls emptied, we stood staring at each other.

"Do I have to tell you," Sonya said, all-too-quietly, "whose car it is that has those scratches?

She didn't. I knew. And, in her expression, I saw that she knew I knew.

"And do I have to guess how you got that messed-up eye?"

The bell rang; kids began to disappear into classrooms. I slowly shook my head. No.

"Is there more?"

The hallway was empty now. Wordlessly, I lifted my shirt, let her study my torso. She looked at it, face immobile.

"How much worse does it have to get, Shan?"

I didn't know. All I knew was, at that moment, it felt like things couldn't get any worse than they already were.

Little did we know.

Chapter 14

The day crawled by, like something leaving a trail of slime behind it.

Sonya didn't look at me or talk to me again, leaving an increasingly bewildered Zip to play go-between during Science, and looking at both of us with an expression of hurt bewilderment, when we answered him in toneless monosyllables. We had a pop quiz on the first week's material; I couldn't have flunked it more spectacularly if I'd tried.

Language Arts, and Kallie was there, suddenly filling my vision, overwhelming me with her smell. She took my arm and pulled me down into my seat, seating herself next to me, and then giving me a big, juicy kiss that caused half the room to exhale: "Awww." I couldn't help but sneak a look at Sonya, but she was very fixedly staring out the window, not looking at us. Mr Graves said, "Now, Shannon, down boy!" and a few kids laughed at me, the sexual aggressor, the dominant one. Kallie just smiled meaningfully: it was a smile that said, "I know better."

We were discussing a poem by Ezra Pound, called "And the days are not full enough." Mr Graves read it aloud, slowly, accompanied by the sound of some twelve cell phones slowly being shut down.

> *And the days are not full enough*
> *And the nights are not full enough*
> *And life slips by like a field mouse*
> *Not shaking the grass.*

Mr Graves let the last words hang in the air for a moment, like a scaffold full of nooses, as he surveyed the class. "Comments, anyone?"

"I think it's about the briefness of life," Kallie said, unexpectedly. She hadn't spoken much that week in English: she'd mostly just smiled at me, and occasionally doodled little drawings on my paper. Now, however, her words came out with a brisk, almost urgent tone, as though she were one of those students who waved their hand like they were trying to get the attention of someone in a parade.

"How so?" Mr Graves peered at her over his glasses.

"Well," Kallie said, "*obviously,* the days and nights are not enough. Time is slipping by, and the narrator is powerless to do anything about it."

"Okay…" Mr Graves did that slow-pacing thing he did when he was digesting an idea. "But *why?*"

"Why what?" Kallie said, a little impatiently.

"Why is the narrator letting the time slip by?" Mr Graves queried, eyes scanning the room. "Why would someone let their life just pass by, knowing that it's theoretically the only one they have?"

"Unless they're reincarnated," a kid in the back row cracked. There were a couple of snickers.

Mr Graves was unmoved. "Possibly. The point is, if this is the only go-round we get, why is Pound's unnamed narrator so timid?"

"Maybe he's afraid," Sonya said, her voice as clear and forthright as a ringing bell.

"Afraid." Mr Graves raised his eyebrows and smiled a little. "What makes you think that?"

"Well, he talks about a mouse," Sonya said, her eyes locked on the teacher. "It's like that Burns' poem that inspired *Of Mice and Men.* Mice are kind of helpless and pathetic and vulnerable, even if they are cute."

"But it doesn't shake the grass," Kallie rejoined. "It's a survivor."

"Until a predator attacks it," Sonya snapped. (Were they still talking about mice? Sonya's voice was taking on an edge.) "Or it gets stuck in a lab experiment."

"You're a lab experiment," Kallie snarled, eyes blazing. I recognized that look.

"Ladies, ladies," Mr Graves said, raising his hands. Sonya and Kallie were openly glaring at each other. The rest of the class seemed to be enjoying the show; several guys looked like they were waiting for the two girls to hit the floor and start tearing at each other's clothing. "Let's not make this personal. Get back to the poem."

Another kid chimed in about all the things he wished he'd done when he was younger and his dad made a lot more money, but now that the dad had been laid off and had to take another job, the family wasn't able to go pet the manta rays in the Bahamas, or something equally stupid. I wasn't listening very hard; I kept focusing on the words Sonya and Kallie had used during their argument, and how both of them seemed to have very determinedly *not* looked at me during it.

The immortal question: was I a man, or a mouse?

At this point, I wasn't entirely sure myself.

*****

"You're eating lunch with me today," Kallie said as we exited class, her hand grabbing mine and pulling me down the hallway. "Don't say no."

"Okay," I said, a bit rattled by all the kids I kept bumping into as she yanked me along.

"You need to meet some other people," she went on, jerking my arm to avoid another collision. "Sierra told me you're still hanging out with those… *guys* from Monday."

"Yeah, so?"

"Not good, Shan," she said, looking at me for the first time since we'd begun this little Bataan Death March. "You're my boyfriend now, you need to think about how what you do affects me; affects both of us."

"Oh," I said. "I'm thinking. Very hard." I was, too. I just didn't know how to ask about her car and Zip.

"Good," she said. We were in front of her Science classroom. She kissed me firmly, pulling my head close to hers with her hands, as if I were in a vise. "Look for me downstairs afterwards."

"Yes'm," I said automatically, as though she were my superior. I regretted it, but she actually smiled, as though she liked me being deferential. She tapped my chest twice with the palm of her hand, and turned to enter class as I had a brief, nightmarish flashback of the night before, when she'd whaled on me in the kitchen.

I was still standing there, looking after her, when people started bumping and pushing into me on their way into the room as the bell rang. I'd been so lost in thought, and had walked so far out of my way, I'd proceeded to make myself late for my own class. Great.

I scurried away down the hall, like a mouse rushing through the grass.

***

In the cafeteria line, I caught Zip's eye as he was exiting, and made a gesture to indicate I was sitting with Kallie at lunch. She was chatting away with Sierra and some football guy who seemed to mostly speak in monosyllables, so she missed Zip's widening eyes and understanding nod.

I was still pretty hungry this morning, so I got a chicken Cesar salad and a roll: safe choices. I followed Kallie and Sierra to a table, the football hunk silently tagging along behind me, and we situated ourselves among six or seven of The Jefferson Academy's Beautiful People, who were already deep in conversation. A couple nodded at Kallie, but a couple others looked through me as if I wasn't even there.

"So, Kal," some guy in a designer skateboard T-shirt said. "This him?"

"This is him," Kallie said. "Shan, this is everybody. Everybody, Shan."

"Right on," the guy said, actually extending a hand to me. I reached for it, but he pulled it away and winked: "No go. Too slow, bro."

"Thanks, Parker. You're a dick," Kallie said loudly, punching his arm. He give her pouty, trembly lips and looked at me sympathetically.

"How'd you get the shiner?" one of the other guys asked, off-handedly.

I didn't dare look at Kallie, who was casually studying her Asian stir-fry. I just shrugged and said, "Bike accident." As I said that, she shifted her eyes and looked at me, with speculation or appreciation. I couldn't tell. The guys nodded sympathetically, and the moment passed.

"So, you swim," a pretty blonde girl with a headband said. "What else should we know about you?"

I shrugged. "Not much to tell." Nothing, at least, I shared with strangers.

"Well, Kallie likes you," headband continued. "You must be doing something right." She and Sierra exchanged looks, as if I were an exception to some unspoken rule.

"He does lots of things right," Kallie said, taking hold of my arm in a possessive way. Fortunately, she was seated on my left, otherwise I wouldn't have been able to eat.

"Ooh, do tell," Sierra purred, looking at me speculatively. I could feel my face flush.

"No, no," K'llie said. "We don't want him getting a swelled head." She smiled at me, but her eyes dared me to contradict her in front of the others. "Let's just say I'm whipping him into shape."

"Try not to leave any scars," headband smirked. I watched, dumbfounded, as Kallie coolly picked up her water glass and hurled it in the other girl's face.

She let out a wail: "You *bitch!*"

"Oh, go wash yourself," Kallie said, tossing her a pile of napkins. She looked nettled, as though the headband chick had been the one causing problems. "Seriously, Sofia, get a life."

"Look who's talking," Sofia hissed, makeup running down her face, as Sierra helped her gather her sodden lunch and they stomped away together. A couple of guys at the table clapped and whistled as they went.

"You got yourself a spitfire here," one of the football guys said, nodding at Kallie, but addressing me. "I'd think carefully about pissing her off."

"I do," I said, shoveling my salad into my mouth. I wanted to get away from this table as soon as possible. The atmosphere seemed so casually cruel, it was toxic. Kallie squeezed my arm again; as a "thank you" or a warning, I couldn't tell.

"There you go," the football guy from the line said. "Don't make waves, and everything's good. 'S not that hard."

"Says the man with a 1.5 GPA," another jock-type said. This incited more slugging amongst them; it was like eating with three-year-olds. I couldn't help but reflect how comparatively nicbriskete it was hanging out with Sonya and Zip, and how they bantered with each other without being mean about it. Everyone at this table seemed to be jockeying for position, and being mean was the way to go about getting it. They may have had nicer clothes than some of the kids at other schools I'd attended, but contrary to what the Corcorans implied, the other night, these sure as hell weren't a better class of kids.

I tried not to wince as I kept hearing the sound of fists connecting with various arms, torsos, and backs. Just Then, a TWEEEEEET! sound cut through the din. Coach Tsai was looming over our table, whistle in one hand. Apparently, he was working lunch duty.

"*Gentlemen*...and lady!" he boomed, nodding at Kallie. "Everything all right here?"

There were a few mumbled "Yeahs" from the end of the table.

"Then I suggest you dump your trash and get to class," Coach continued. "NOW."

It was a mass exodus. Everyone arose, grumbling under their breath, and grabbed their trays, though some of the guys deliberately left their milk containers and stained napkins on the table, calling back "It's not my mess!" when Coach barked after them.

"Well, that could've been better," Kallie said, stacking our trays and standing. I shoved another couple forkfuls of salad into my mouth and grabbed my roll, lest it got tossed in the trash with everything else. I didn't want to keep sitting alone at an empty table, especially a trashed one that had Coach Tsai pretty steamed. As we passed him, while he was gathering stained napkins and use milk cartons, he called out acidly, "Thank you *so* much for your kindness and responsibility, future leaders of America."

"Should I go back and help him?" I asked, looking behind me as the coach gathered up the detritus left behind by our lunch table.

"That's what they pay him for," Kallie said impatiently, dragging me out. At a far-off table, I caught a glimpse of Sonya and Zip — and, surprisingly, Theo from the swim team — eating together. Theo looked surprised and Zip gave me a pitying look, but Sonya just slowly shook her head, as though she couldn't comprehend what she was seeing.

I couldn't help but make a mental note: this was the third meal I'd had with Kallie that had ended with drama, and me not getting enough to eat.

"So, tonight," Kallie said as she pulled me along. "I think you should have me over for dinner."

I was so surprised, I almost stumbled, but caught myself. "Huh?"

"Oh, you're cute when you're speechless," Kallie said, putting her forefinger against my lips and stroking them. "But we've been at my house the last two nights, I think I should meet your mother. And she can cook for us."

For some reason, this idea did not fill me with delight.

"That would be great," I said. "But she's working tonight." Actually, the odds were pretty good that she would be working at least part of the evening; however, she might be home around eight, if she was off-shift first. But I had this weird feeling in my gut that seized up when I thought about Kallie walking around our rental house, looking at our threadbare furniture, sizing everything up with that calculating, judgmental eye. I didn't feel comfortable having her there; it was almost like she would mess with the energy, or something. But how was I going to explain that? For all I knew, she'd use my mom's absence as a reason to come over, anyways.

As if she had telepathy, Kallie frowned. "Hmmm. Well, that's annoying. What if I came over just until she gets home?"

"I really have to catch up on homework," I said, truthfully. "I totally bombed that quiz earlier today." As her face began to darken at my refusal, I added hurriedly, "But you'll definitely meet my mom at the swim meet on Saturday morning. You can talk with her then."

"Well," she said, running her fingers fixedly along her binder, "I *guess* that would be okay. I should probably do some homework as well. Maybe we can plan something special for tomorrow night?"

"Tomorrow would be great," I said, relieved. I kissed her, and for once there wasn't passion or danger or heat in it — it was just friendly. "Let's talk then."

"Oh, I'll call you tonight to check in," she said, looking right at me. "Make sure you're home and being a good boy."

"Aren't I always?" I said, trying to smile.

She didn't answer. She just looked me up and down, scrutinizing my face as though she were trying to look for clues to a mystery, something that she couldn't solve, but was bothering her.

Then she went into class, leaving me once again alone in a hallway surrounded by hundreds of people.

Chapter 15

I did better at practice, but still not as well as I'd done on my first day. After I swam the relay, I noticed both coaches looking at me with somewhat concerned expressions, and talking among themselves. This really didn't help my confidence, and I was even more taciturn in the locker room afterwards, blowing off the shower and just putting my clothes on for the bike ride home. I was done talking to people.

I fell off my bike, I said over and over to various guys in the locker room before practice. Seriously, it's no big deal. It hardly hurts at all. Yeah, bike accident. Totally sucks. Coach Corcoran, examining my bruises as I pulled my shirt on, making a tch-tch sound as he shook his head: "Be more careful, Shan. First meet tomorrow: we don't want to lose you right out of the box."

The excuse I'd offered Kallie had actually become the truth: I needed to be alone, to catch up on my homework, and just to think.

The sun was popping in and out of the clouds, but it was still warm. I biked slowly, feeling my muscles extend and contract, and tried not to think about last night. *Your girlfriend beat you up,* my brain whispered against my will. *She totally turned you into a punching bag, and you let it happen. You didn't even fight back. What's wrong with you?*

Again unbidden, memories of Frankie popped into my brain. Memories of being grabbed, being shaken, being thrown against the wall, of the slaps and punches that rained down on me whenever I was too noisy, too whiny, too questioning, too in the way. There was one friend I'd brought home in third grade to play with, who'd wound up fleeing our then-apartment, wide-eyed with terror, when Frankie came home in a foul mood from a bad day at work and started in yelling and throwing stuff. The only good thing about days like that was Frankie was a lot less likely to slap my mom.

I tried to make Frankie disappear from my mental vision as I chained my bike to our porch and unlocked the front door. Sometimes, when I was home alone, I felt so restless I wanted to jump out of my skin, and I liked to listen to loud music and bounce around like a crazy fool; but other days I just liked to flop down on our ancient, threadbare purple couch, and read some science-fiction for a couple hours. The only TV show I liked to watch in the evening was "Family Feud." It was always fun watching people trying to match their answers to the hundred people surveyed, and see how completely wrong they could be. Everything else on TV seemed to be cops standing over bodies.

I made some mac-and-cheese — dinner of champions — with hot dogs diced into it for extra protein, and some green beans, and got down to my homework. It was around seven and I was on the last page of my history questions when my phone rang. "Hello?"

"What're you doing right now?" Zip asked. I heard giggling in the background.

"Just finishing my homework. Why?"

"Oh good," he said. The phone went dead, and the doorbell rang. I shook my head in confusion, like a dog getting out of a lake and trying to shake himself dry, then went and opened the front door. Zip and Sonya were standing there, smirking.

"Hey!" I said, surprised and genuinely happy.

"Hey yourself," Sonya said, grinning. "Can we come in?"

"Sure!" I said, before thinking better of it. "Come on in." Zip and Sonya stepped inside, Zip carrying a huge knapsack slung over one shoulder, Sonya a canvas grocery bag. Zip tossed his bounty on the couch, and he and Sonya stood, looking at me expectantly.

"So this is — uh, our home," I said, trying to remember how people welcomed others to their houses in movies. I spread my arms to show off our dwelling, but considering the living room bled into the dining room at a right angle, and neither was much bigger than a basketball court key, there wasn't a lot to see. My mom did her best by filling the window shelves with cheap plants she got at farmers' markets that tended to vine, and she'd painted a Venice street scene on the living room wall to match the one on the jar in her bedroom. We'd inherited my grandmother's ancient dining room table and buffet, so the dining room had some shabby elegance. At least the place was clean.

"I love the mural," Sonya said, touching my arm and smiling at me. Some people might have done that and it would've seemed patronizing, but she was looking at the artwork with genuine appreciation. "Your mom do that?"

"Yeah," I said, a little embarrassed but appreciative.

"Holy shit," Zip said, impressed. "Venice, right? I could tell, 'cause it has a river running through it."

"They're called canals," Sonya said, rolling her eyes at me. "They use gondolas. Are your parents wasting their money on your tuition?"

"Probably," Zip said, cheerfully. "Definitely wasted it on the ballet lessons."

The image of Zip as a child in a tutu got me giggling, and then Sonya joined in; it didn't help when Zip, with a mock-offended look, sank into a plié.

"Enough of this," Zip said when our hysteria had died down. "We decided to surprise you with entertainment."

"And treats," Sonya said, pulling out a container of ice cream and waving it at me.

I was so stunned, I could barely move or speak. Aside from the neighbor who let me use his pool to practice, I couldn't remember the last time someone other than my mom had done something nice for me.

"You said you've never seen *Harold and Maude*," Zip went on, stepping into the silence and unzipping his bag. "Unacceptable."

"But we don't have a Blu-Ray player," I said apologetically. The only reason we even had a DVD player was via a church rummage sale.

"No worries," Zip said, pulling a fistful of cords out of his bag as Sonya started to unpack ice cream, whipped cream, and assorted toppings and put them on the dining room table. "I have a Netflix account, I brought my laptop, and an LCD projector. All I need from you is some good speakers. Or if you don't have them, we can just listen off the laptop."

"I have speakers," I said, almost burbling with happiness. I went and disconnected them from the stereo in my room. By the time I was back, Zip already had the projector perched on a plant stand, banishing my mom's Christmas cactus to the bookshelf. He had everything set up in less than five minutes, projecting the white screen onto the opposite wall of the living room without the mural.

"So what is this about?" I asked, as Zip finished popping cords into place and the speakers suddenly giving a loud crackle as they sprang to life. Sonya arrived, arms laden with bowls filled with ice cream sundaes, and distributed them to all of us as we all flopped on the couch.

"It's a love story," Sonya said, "about a suicidal nineteen-year-old boy and an eighty-year old woman."

"What the *what?*" I said, none-too-eloquently.

"Ssshh," Zip said, as the screen filled with a pair of shoes walking down a staircase. "Just go with it."

I went with it, but if you've never seen *Harold and Maude*, it's very hard to explain what it's like. About ten minutes in, during a third onscreen suicide attempt, I turned to Sonya and said, "What the hell *is* this movie?"

"It's about love," Sonya said, patting my arm firmly.

So far, it didn't seem to be about love at all, but I kept watching. And slowly, the movie got funnier and funnier, and wilder and wilder. By the time we reached the scene with an unfortunate date involving Harold and a pretentious actress, we were screaming with laughter.

"I think this is one of the funniest things I've ever seen," I said.

"Wait till the ending," Zip murmured.

"ZIP!" Sonya actually reached around me to hit him. Zip curled into an apologetic ball.

"Wait till the ending," indeed. The movie finished, and I just sat there, stunned, tears rolling down my face, as Cat Stevens sang one more song.

"Good?" Zip enquired.

"That was freaking amazing," I said, wiping my eyes. I didn't even feel embarrassed about reacting to the movie in front of them. Sonya's eyes were glistening, too.

"I told you it was about love," she said, smiling.

"Well—"

"It is," she insisted. "We get all hung up on what we think love is, or what it should be like. But when it happens — really happens — it's not what we expect."

I pondered that for a moment while I took the ice cream bowls to the kitchen. As I was doing that my mom came home, so I let her say hi to Sonya and Zip while Zip was dismantling the electronics, and I washed up the dishes. *What is love?* I wondered, as I quickly spun a scrub brush around the hot fudge stains at the bottom of the bowl.

"Hi, honey," my mom said, kissing my hair and taking off her coat. Apparently, she wasn't still mad about this morning and the 'bike accident.'

"Sonya and Zip surprised me," I said. "Hope that's okay." From the living room, I could hear shrieks of laughter as Sonya and Zip cracked up over who-knew-what.

"Okay?" She smiled at me tiredly. "You having friends over? That's very okay."

"Yo, Shan-Man!" Zip called. My mom raised her eyebrows, delighted at Zip's having bestowed a nickname on me. I scowled at her amusement and returned to the living room. "You guys outie?"

"Off like a prom dress," Sonya said, giving me a huge hug and a quick kiss on my cheek. I blushed beet-red. Zip slapped my hand and gave me a side-hug. "See you tomorrow?"

"Definitely," I said. "Thanks so much, that was really awesome."

"We knew you'd like it," Zip said happily. "You're one of us, remember?" And then it was as though he'd said too much, or the wrong thing, and a shadow crossed his face. Sonya shot him the world's fastest glare, and picked up her bag. "So, tomorrow?"

"Tomorrow," I said. I opened the door for them, and they waved as they walked down the street to Sonya's car.

"They're so nice," my mom practically burbled as I closed the door. "I knew you'd make some friends at this school!"

"Yes, I made some friends," I said indulgently, putting the plant and furniture back where they belonged. "They're kind of awesome."

"They really are," she agreed. "And this Saturday I'll finally meet Kallie, right?"

"*Yes,* Mother. Saturday."

"Don't do the Norman Bates voice with me," my mom said, giving me a gentle shove. She hates it when I get overly formal and call her "Mother," especially when I make my eyes look all crazy. At that moment, the phone rang. I grabbed it, thinking it was Zip or Sonya and they forgot something.

"Hey."

"Hey," Kallie said coolly.

I almost dropped the receiver. "Hey!" I responded, flustered. All of a sudden, my heart sped up.

"How's it going?" she asked, a little too casually.

"Good," I said. "Really good. I got a lot of homework done. You?"

"I did some stuff," she said carefully.

"Yeah?" I was having problems keeping my voice from wobbling. My mom poked her head around from the kitchen, eyebrows raised quizzically. I mouthed "Kallie" at her, and she nodded.

"Uh-huh," she said. "So, your homework is good. What else did you do tonight?"

"Watched some TV." True, as far as that went.

"Oh, that's nice."

Something about the way she was choosing her words made the hairs on the back of my neck tingle. Some instinct deep in my brain had me stroll surreptitiously to the window and look out, as if I were staring at my reflection. A couple houses down from ours, I could see a BMW parked at the curb, engine running and lights on, but I couldn't tell what color it was or who was in it. Nonetheless, my heart jumped into my throat.

"So," I said. My voice cracked.

"So," she said pleasantly. "Guess I'll see you in the morning?"

"Yeah!" I said, desperately cheerful. "See you then!"

"All right then." CLICK.

I stood, frozen, watching the car with the lights. It didn't move.

"Sweetie," my mom said, starting to re-enter the living room, "I—"

"Sshh," I said automatically, raising a finger to stop her from coming closer.

"What is it?" my mom said, her voice suddenly quivering with concern. "Do you see something?"

I flicked my eyes at her, saw her standing in the kitchen doorway, clutching a dish towel, twisting it in her hands, fear in her eyes. I remembered that look. I'd seen it many, many times in my life. I should've known better than to scare her like this.

As I flicked my eyes back to the window, the car's headlights came on full, and it pulled away into the darkness.

"It's nothing," I said, turning away from the window and working very deliberately to keep my voice on an even keel. "Just thought I saw something weird outside."

"What weird?" Mom said, taking a step towards me, her anxious eyes searching my face.

I shrugged.

"Do you still think you see Frankie sometimes?" Mom asked, sitting down at the table with sudden weariness. "I have moments where I think I do."

I did too, even though this wasn't one of them. But it provided the perfect out. "Yeah, once in a while."

"I just remind myself," she said, taking a sip from her mug, "that that's all over. We're safe now."

"Yeah," I said, uncertainly. Safe. The word made me think of a big, heavy thing you put valuables in, and spun the combination. Nothing got in. Or out.

"I'm going to bed," I said, a little abruptly. Mom nodded. I turned off the light in the living room and left her there, only the dining room light above her, holding her mug and staring at the wall.

I went to my room, re-attached my speakers, and got undressed. I lay down on the bed, staring into the darkness for a few minutes, then got up and turned on my computer did a web search under 'Cat Stevens.' Sure enough, the song from the movie was there.

"Well if you want to sing out, sing out
And if you want to be free, be free
Cause there's a million ways to be
You know that there are..."

I sat naked at my desk and listened to the song all the way through, and thought about love, and freedom, and what kind of people show up at your house with a movie and ice cream, just because they could, just because they wanted to share something with you. "Because you're one of us."

The question, more than ever, was: should I be?

Chapter 16

The next morning I waited for Kallie in the school lobby, but she texted me and said she was running late. I'd been feeling anxious all morning, wondering what I was going to say when I saw her, but I wound up not even having to worry about it. When I saw Zip and Sonya arrive, the first thing Sonya did was wail at me in a fluted voice, *'Harold! That was your last date!'"* And we all lost it and laughed ourselves crazy, while people stared at us. It was nice way to start the morning.

Kallie showed up one minute before English started. She didn't look at anyone else; just walked in and gave me a huge kiss, her fingernails digging briefly into the sides of my neck, and whispered, "I missed you." I responded in kind, despite Mr Graves' admonishing look. She sat down and wrapped her fingers around my arm like a boa constrictor, thus severely hampering my ability to take notes. Fortunately, today we were watching a video on "What is Poetry?" so I didn't have to write very much. Whenever I'd pull a bit on her arm due to taking notes, she pulled me that much closer and tighter, her eyes staring at me.

Kallie had some sort of Leadership lunch meeting, where they were ordering pizza, so I was free to have lunch with my friends, though she warned me, while leaving English class, as she ran her fingers along my shoulders and the back of my neck, "You *will* check in with me at three thirty before practice, right, honey?" Steel and nectar. That was Kallie.

"Of course," I said. She kissed me again and lightly slapped the side of my face as she walked away.

"So, I've been thinking," Zip said, biting into a limp bean burrito and chewing thoughtfully. "You need to have a proper meal before your first meet tomorrow."

"I hope that's not part of it," I said, nodding at the sad burrito.

"Nope," Zip said, mouth full, wiping ranchero sauce off his fingers. "Eating this is so we *appreciate* the proper meal. You up for my place tonight?"

"I'd love to," I said, eyeing my sad Asian noodle bowl with contempt. Kallie had said she wasn't allowed to bring me any leftover pizza, and the memory of the bagel sandwiches Zip had brought us the day before was still lingering in my mind. "But I imagine Kallie will probably want to do something, though."

"Bring her with you," Zip said, completely straight-faced.

I almost dropped my fork. He burst into giggles, and turned pink. "Oh man, if you could've *seen* your face…"

"Talk about the serpent amongst the doves," Sonya murmured, her mouth full of yogurt.

"What's that mean?"

"It's from the Bible. Matthew: 'Be as shrewd as serpents, and as innocent as doves.'"

"I think she's calling your girlfriend a snake," Zip said, not-so-helpfully. "Not that we don't really, *really* like her. Down deep."

"Like *Journey to the Center of the Earth*," Sonya intoned. Her face looked as if it were carved out of stone, except for a tiny smile tugging at the corners of her mouth in reaction to her own joke.

"Here's the deal," Zip said. "We'll wait for you after practice. It'll be short, because of the meet tomorrow — they always are, the day before. So we'll look for you around five, and then we'll go to my family's for Shabbat supper. It wraps around nine, and you can tell Kallie you'll see her after, for a late-nighter."

"Well, maybe," I said, feeling somewhat doubtful. I was still wondering about the accident with Zip, and whether Kallie's bumper was really scratched up with paint from Zip's bike. And the car I'd seen the previous night… On the other hand, a late night with Kallie had a stronger possibility of ending up in sex. It was almost pathetic how easily I could be manipulated by that opportunity.

"Just ask her," Zip said. "Real nice."

"Don't ask," Sonya interjected, raising a warning finger. "*Tell* her this is the way it's going to be."

"I don't think that happens very often with her," I said, tentatively.

"No better time to start," Sonya said, looking at me meaningfully. "And you might want to ask her, oh-so-casually, about those paint scratches on her bumper?" Damn, could she read me? I might as well have lit up my brain like a neon sign.

Zip, bless his heart, wasn't listening to any of this. He was already on his phone with his mom, saying things like *corned beef* and *brisket.* This boded well.

***

At three thirty, I was standing by the door to the gym when Kallie appeared. She walked right up to me, put her hand behind my head to pull it down to her, and kissed me hungrily. "*God,* I've wanted that for hours," she breathed.

I tried not to become overly aroused: I was going to have to go in the locker room and strip in a few minutes. Her pressure against my upper body reminded me that I still had some bruises healing under my shirt, but I jumped at the opportunity to take charge. "So, what are your plans for tonight?"

"Being with you, lover," she purred, her hands wandering across my chest, along my spine. She actually squeezed my butt. A couple kids walking by openly snickered, but she didn't seem to care. Her lips brushed my neck, then my ears. "I need to go do some shopping for a bit, though, and find an outfit so I can look spec-*tac*-ular at your meet tomorrow. Can you keep yourself busy if practice ends early?"

And lo, the heavens opened.

"That's perfect," I said, trying not to sound too eager. "I've got dinner plans, but then I can meet up with you later."

"Dinner plans?" The soft, seductive Kallie disappeared. A hard tone came into her voice, a glint of samurai sword flickered in her eyes. "Who with?"

I thought about lying and saying the team was going to do something, but that would've been too easy for her to check. I decided on straight honesty, but my voice might have quavered a tiny bit as I spoke. "Zip invited me to dinner with his family after practice. But he said we'll be done around nine or so."

"*He* said that," Kallie said, giving me a look of contempt. "Don't you mean *she*? Or *it*?" I was just opening my mouth to defend Zip and ask her not to talk like that, but all of a sudden her perturbed expression vanished, like a quick summer shower. Instead, her eyes glittered, and her mouth stretched into a too-wide smile. "You know what? Fine. That's fine. You can have your little meal with your friends. But I think we need some dessert."

"I like dessert," I said, leaning in for another kiss. Her lips didn't pucker.

"I do, too," she said, still smiling. "I hear this restaurant Catch has *excellent* cheesecake."

A warning bell should've been ringing in my head. Catch, where my mom worked? The coffee shop was one thing, but Catch was a whole 'nother level. On the other hand, they'd probably let me have my mom's discount without her being there, since she'd be off work by nine.

"And," Kallie continued, noticing my brief hesitation, "maybe we could get that cheesecake to go, and take it up to a room in The Excelsior?" She looked right at me, eyes glittering, as she ran her hand over the front of my pants. "You get dessert. I'll get the room."

There were so many things wrong with this plan, I could barely keep up with them all. She wanted to go to my mom's place of employment for dessert. She wanted to get a room at the hotel. I could be recognized by anyone there at any time. This should've been a sea of cautionary red flags, something in my brain yelling, *Slow down, Stop, Not a good idea!!*

But another part of me was remembering the four-poster beds in the Excelsior's rooms, the starchy sheets and the thick comforters, the full-length old-style mirrors, the oversized bathtubs. And knowing Kallie, she'd agree to all of it. And this time, there'd be no distractions. No dinner with parents, no brother, no scary drawer — nothing to ruin the experience.

And maybe this time, *I'd* finally be in control.

She must have misinterpreted my reverie as hesitation because she stepped back again, and I noticed the flash of anger cross her face. "If it's a *problem* being with me…"

"No, no!" I panicked, my voice almost jumped an octave and cracked. Right at that moment, wouldn't you know it, Theo approached the locker room door, turning at the sound of my voice. He grinned at me and started to raise his hand in greeting, as if to touch my hand or my shoulder, but then realized who was in front of me, and openly flinched and jerked away.

Kallie had spun like a rattlesnake at Theo's presence, but he opened the door and quickly scooted inside. In a flash, I had my hand on her arm, turning her back towards me. "We can absolutely do that," I said, covering my nervousness with bravado. "My mom's off work by nine, so I'll meet you there. We can start dessert in the restaurant, then…" I swallowed, and my throat went a little dry. Shit. Was I always fated to feel like a little kid at moments like this? "We can take the rest upstairs."

"Oh, baby," she said, her finger playing insistently with my nipple as she kissed me again. "We like it when you follow orders." She nipped my neck, then pulled reluctantly away, pouting. "Maybe I'll get a special outfit for tonight, too," she said. Then she sighed, almost regretfully as she turned away. "Of course, we're just going to wind up taking it off…"

I had to change clothes in the bathroom stall of the locker room, and wait five minutes for my erection to subside. Damn her.

***

"Shabbat shalom!" Zip yelled as we entered the front of his family's restaurant and deli, Knish/Nosh.

"Shabbat shalom, my darling," a middle-aged woman with dark brown hair and sparkling eyes said, coming from around the deli counter and throwing open her arms. She had a turquoise-blue apron on that showed a bagel and some other baked good sitting on a park bench enjoying sandwiches while wearing little yarmulkes. She was pretty but her face and body had a softness to it, as if they were molded out of challah dough.

She folded Zip into her arms and gave him a huge kiss. Unlike most high school kids I'd known, Zip hugged and kissed her back. "This is Shan."

"Oh, Shan! We've heard such wonderful things about you," Zip's mother said. She opened her arms, and before I knew it I was swept up into a hug, too. She smelled like cooking and pickling spices, but it was a nice, homey smell. I had a wave of strange feelings overwhelm me, as I compared it to the flowery smell of my mom, and the odd lack of smell from Kallie's mother.

165

"Thank you," I said, awkwardly. Sonya smiled at me, enjoying my nervousness. The place was sensational — or maybe I should say *gvaldik*. (Zip had to translate that for me.) On the walls were autographed pictures of famous entertainers and sports figures, and the tablecloths all had beautiful Hebrew lettering stitched on them, but were then covered by plastic tabletops to protect them. The walls were all blue and white, and had the Star of David prominently featured. One section had a long deli counter filled with drool-worthy smoked meats; jars of chicken soup and Russian borsht; baked goods, such as rugelach and hamantasch (it took me weeks for Zip to teach me how to pronounce those words correctly, too); black-and-white cookies; plates of knishes; containers of rice pudding, and the like. The back wall was nothing but wire baskets, in which a last few orphan bagels lay abandoned and unwanted. The deli counter took care of quick orders and to-go items, kind of like the coffee shop at The Excelsior, and the rest of the restaurant was for dine-in. They closed at four, so the family could have nights off, or — on Fridays — host Shabbat dinner.

Before I knew it, Zip's mom had turned out the CLOSED sign on the door, and was ushering Zip, Sonya, and me past the kitchen entrance, through some heavy dark-blue draperies, and then, all of a sudden, we were in the private dining room. Unlike the main part of the restaurant, which had black-and-white pictures of people like Woody Allen, Barbra Streisand and Sandy

Koufax, the walls in here had what looked like hand-made watercolors, decorated with more Hebrew writing. There were also bronze and silver candlesticks and figures placed on a raised shelf, high around the room. In the center of the room, which had very dim lights, was an enormous round table with a Lazy Susan the size of a merry-go-round, and the table was absolutely overflowing with amazing-looking food, presumably made that afternoon or taken out of the case.

"Don't get to thinking you're special," Zip whispered. "We're not supposed to cook on Friday nights, so they tend to throw a whole bunch of leftovers out to nosh on."

"Zip — such a smack I'll give you!" Zip's mother did, in fact, give Zip a light smack on the shoulder, and then squeezed me again. "We're thrilled you could join us, Shan. Especially after you gave my *zeisele* breakfast the other day. You're some kind of *mentsh*."

"*Oy*, Ma, lay off the Yiddish already," Zip said, almost skipping to the table to survey the spread.

"I didn't make the breakfast," I fumbled. "Not like this."

"We're just so glad you're becoming friends," Mrs Chaiken said, very sincerely. "You know, Zip hasn't always..." The words dribbled away and her eyes suddenly glistened. She bit her lip, and looked at Zip, who was helping himself to a piece of wing from a platter piled high with roast chicken. She looked at me and smiled again, eyes shiny. "We're just very glad he's made a nice new friend."

"What am I, chopped liver?" Sonya said, one arm around Zip's mom. She pronounced it "liv-AH," to Mrs Chaiken's great amusement.

"You," Mrs Chaiken said, taking Sonya's face between her hands so she could plant a kiss on her cheek, "are a *mitzvah* — a gift. Zip, do *not* touch that yet!"

Zip dropped the chicken wing, as though he'd been caught doing something immoral.

"Who said chopped liver?" a voice boomed behind us, and a man entered the dining room with another platter of gorgeous food, followed by a young-ish Filipino guy. (The young guy, Zip explained on the way over, was Charlie Castro: he bussed all the dishes and locked up the restaurant once the family was done eating, so they didn't do any work on the Sabbath and could thus go straight upstairs to relax for the rest of the evening.) Zip's father seemed to be as wide as a barn door and as tall as an elephant, and I couldn't even count how many chins he had. He looked like a man who loved what he did for a living. Behind him, came a girl of about twenty, bearing pitchers of water wine. With her solid build, blonde honey-colored hair, and sauntering walk, she had to be Zip's sister, Rebecca. She smiled at me, like she already knew who I was.

I had the weirdest feeling of being a puzzle piece, locking into a larger pattern that had been waiting for me forever. The feeling of community was overwhelming.

"Sit, sit!" Zip's father was pulling out the chairs, and Rebecca and her mother were already grabbing plates and filling them with food. Zip, Sonya, Charlie, and I pulled out our chairs and slid into our places, me offering an introductory wave at Charlie as I sat. "Shan." He smiled and waved at me, too.

Zip's father had a silver cup at his place, and once everyone had a plateful of food, he chanted over it and sang a prayer to a tune that sounded like it was written using only the black keys of a piano. I didn't know what he was saying, but as someone whose church attendance had been, at best, C & E (Christmas and Easter) for many years, it was kind of neat. While he was singing, Zip's mom lit the candles, suffusing the room with a warm glow.

I looked over at Zip, and realized with a bit of a shock that Zip had somehow acquired a yarmulke, as had his father and Charlie. His eyes were closed and he was helping chant in Hebrew and I had another flash like I'd had that morning. With the candlelight glow and his face in an expression of serenity and prayer, Zip looked— well, beautiful. I wasn't sure if I was supposed to have my eyes closed, or if I should be looking at the tablecloth, the ceiling, or the food, so I kept on looking at Zip's beatific expression, and for just a weird moment, I thought I might start crying.

Sonya was sitting next to me, and she squeezed my hand, as if she could read my thoughts. I squeezed hers back, and she smiled. Then, unbidden, a cold needle of fear pricked into my brain. What would Kallie think if she saw this meal, compared with the dinner at her house? God - only four nights ago! She didn't like Zip and Sonya at all. Sonya was even convinced that she'd tried to scare or hurt Zip intentionally.

Maybe she just needed to get to know them better, I thought. Maybe I can figure out a way that they can sit together tomorrow during the meet. If she could only see them through my eyes, wouldn't she know they were good people? How could she not? Wasn't it obvious? *When people show you who they are, believe them.* I'd read that quote from Maya Angelou, somewhere.

And yet, I suddenly realized, as the prayers finished and everyone dug into their plates with merry enthusiasm, that was exactly what I *wasn't* doing with Kallie. I kept seeing her as an idealized, better self that I figured was inside of her, and glossing over any evidence to the contrary.

I made up my mind, there amidst the candlelight's glow and the laughter and the *clink* of china and glassware: Kallie and I were going to have to have a serious talk tonight over that cheesecake.

Chapter 17

After dinner, we went upstairs to Zip's apartment for an hour, so he could show me how to play *Lord of the Rings* on his Xbox.

"You're pretty good at this," I said, as yet another Orc turned me into his lunch.

"I am," Zip said proudly. "I'm one bad-ass Legolas with this bow, let me tell you."

"In what universe are you Orlando Bloom?" Sonya queried from behind us, where she was laid out on the couch, listening to one of Zip's father's ancient Ella Fitzgerald CD's, *Sings the Cole Porter Songbook*. She was also leafing through some gigantic tome that appeared to be an overview of the history of languages worldwide.

"In the same universe that you're Beyoncé," Zip parried, never taking his eyes off the screen. *Zzzzzzwap!!* A cascade of arrows went raining down upon the enemy. The carnage was extensive.

"Well," I said, reluctantly putting down my controller. "I should probably head out. I'm supposed to be at The Excelsior around nine."

"The Excelsior?" Sonya looked at me as though an Orc were lurking behind me with a pickaxe. "Why are you going there?"

For sex, I didn't say. I thought fast, and decided to tell just enough of the truth so that it wasn't technically lying. "For dessert. Kallie wants to try the cheesecake at Catch."

"Mmm-hmm," Sonya said, looking at me very significantly. "Well, don't do anything I wouldn't do."

"You wouldn't touch Kallie Corcoran with a twenty-foot pole," Zip said, eyes still glued to the TV, still firing one arrow after the other. He was actually breaking into a sweat.

"This is true," Sonya said. She kissed her fingers and brought them to my cheek without getting up from the couch. As I leaned down to her, Zip gave me a half-hug around the leg with his free arm.

"Thanks for dinner," I said.

"Remember, your dead body turns up on Instagram, we warned you," Sonya murmured darkly.

"Charming," I said, a little nettled. I supposed I should've been grateful she was letting me go at all, but it still rankled.

"We nag because we care," Zip sang. "So, see you at school tomorrow morning?"

"School?" I'd gone blank.

"You have a swim meet at eight o'clock," Sonya said, exasperated. "Good Lord, Zip, what are we going to do with this child? It's a miracle he doesn't need Velcro shoes."

"I'm fine," I said, heading for the door. "My shoes are fine, dinner was fine, I'm fine, everything's fine." I opened it, then turned back to them — somewhat theatrically, I admit, but I had the perfect zinger loaded. "I'm not a brainiac like you, Sonya, but I don't *need* to know trig, or speak Sanskrit."

I thought that would put her in her place, but she just smiled at me and blew me another kiss. "Sanskrit is only a written language, darling."

Fudge, fudge, fudge, fudge, *fudge*. I closed the don their laughter.

***

Friday night, the Excelsior had a jazz combo playing at Catch, and the crowds could get thick. I expected I might have to wait for a table, but Mina, the hostess on duty, walked right up to me past the other parties waiting in the lobby and gave me a kiss on the cheek. (It was not like it sounded—she was old enough to be my aunt, and had known me since elementary school.) "Hi, Shan, baby. Your girl's already here."

My girl, I thought, getting a little chilly-willy of a shudder on the back of my neck — from anticipation or nervousness, I wasn't sure. Mina walked me over an aisle, past all the chattering customers, and sure enough, there was Kallie, tucked in one of the little booths for two. She was wearing a black dress and boots, and her hair was down. She looked sensational, if a bit Mafia-daughter. "*There* you are," she said, just as she had the other day when I'd met her by the pool, her tone implying that she'd been waiting awhile.

"Am I late?" I'd texted her as I'd left Zip's, and had expected her to meet me at Catch by nine thirty, which it just was.

"No, but I was early," Kallie said, her eyes wandering over me like emerald spiders. "How was your— dinner?"

"Fine," I said, ignoring the steel in her voice. "Zip's family has a deli, so we did the Friday night Shabbat meal and then hung out for a bit."

"Was the food as good as at my house?" She actually asked that.

"No," I said, lying. Why get into it? Actually, considering the last time I'd been to her house and I'd wound up not eating anything, I thought this was kind of a nervy question on her part. "Is this the new outfit?"

"You like?" she purred, moving her head just so, so the candlelight caught her dangly silver earrings and made them shine.

"Yeah." Boy, was I eloquent.

"I got something for you, too," she said, letting the words slide around like butter on a warm skillet. She patted the bag next to her. "But all in good time, my pretty. All in good time. Didn't you promise me some cheesecake?"

"It's very good here," I said, my throat suddenly turning into the Gobi Desert. I remembered what she'd said about getting dessert to go. "Did you still, uh…?"

"You *are* a hungry boy," she said, flashing one of those there-and-gone smiles. The waiter — a guy with tattooed forearms whom I didn't know very well, one of those types who's just doing this till his band takes off — suddenly appeared, and Kallie focused all of her radiance and attention on him, leaving me feeling like the far side of Mercury. "We've decided to split a slice of cheesecake to go. Just put it in a box with some forks and we'll take it upstairs."

"Very good," the guy said, nodding and removing the menus. I couldn't help but notice she didn't say "thank you." It was just business as usual when someone provided her a service. Based on my mom's background, I was a little sensitive about these things.

As if she had ESP, Kallie said, "So, tomorrow will I finally get to meet your mother at the meet?"

"Yeah, of course," I said, caught off-guard.

"Good," she said briskly. "I feel like you've been keeping me from interacting with people this week."

I was keeping *her* from interacting with people?

"I'd never," she went on musingly, "want to feel like you're hiding our relationship. But I don't get to be with you at school — not really — and I haven't met your family yet." She looked over my shoulder, as though she were trying to figure this out by staring at a distant blackboard diagram.

I felt like I was in Bizarro World. Kallie had kept me on a tight leash all that week, and now she was acting like I was the one keeping her from the other important people in my life. Had we passed through the Looking-Glass?

"No," I said, stalling. "I'm not... it's just that I know you don't like Sonya and Zip much, and my mom usually works nights."

"Here," Kallie said, eyes sweeping the room. She just stated the fact: here.

"Yeah."

"So, your mom works here, and your dad's— not in the picture." Kallie's eyes locked back on me, and seemed to want to penetrate into my soul. "And you swim."

"And I swim," I echoed weakly. I was getting that sick, nervous feeling again.

"Anything else I should know?"

"No," I lied.

"You know I can find things out," she said with no inflection in her voice, but her eyes were cool and unfathomable. "You don't have to hide things from me."

"What about you?" I parried, trying not to sound irritated. "You keep things from me all the time."

"Nothing important," she said coolly.

"And," I said, "I was the one who had to explain to people on the swim team — including your uncle — why my body was bruised up today."

"What did you say?" Kallie asked, not sounding very concerned.

"That I fell off my bike."

"Ah." She eyed the candle for a moment, then flicked her eyes back at me. "Sorry about that, I got a little upset when you puked all over me in the kitchen." Her voice was level, but a hint of accusation lay beneath the surface, like something that could bite you if you ventured in much deeper.

"I didn't mean to," I said, off-guard. Why were we suddenly talking about my faults again?

"Well, now I know," she said briskly. "I won't feed you peppers, and it won't happen *ever* again. Right?"

"Right," I said, weakly.

"Speaking of food," she continued, swiveling the conversation as neatly as a peg in a socket, "how long does it take them to box up some freaking cheesecake? I'm going to go use the restroom and see if I can track down that useless waiter." She scooted out of the booth, then bent down and kissed my neck, her hair draping against my cheek. She smelled intoxicating, like a blend of different tropical perfumes all designed to make you want to take off your clothes as soon as possible. Her breath was warm. "Be right back."

I watched her go, and sure enough, she buttonholed the waiter right as he was pouring water for another table. I watched with a mixture of embarrassment and admiration as she put her hand on his arm and leaned in, just as she had with me a few seconds before, and said something I couldn't hear but made him flush and hurry away. She looked back at me and actually smiled a little before heading towards the restroom.

Left alone, I found myself looking at the old couple again several booths over — the one I'd watched on Monday night — and how the old man was holding his wife's ancient hand while they bobbed their heads in time to the music. She rested her head against his shoulder, and I felt a tidal wave of longing and sadness wash over me, as cold and salty as the ocean in winter. When I was with Kallie, I felt charged-up and excited, even intoxicated, but I didn't have that feeling of *safety* that the old couple seemed to have. Safety. Comfort. Love.

I was just beginning to form the question *Do you really love Kallie, and does she really love you?* in my mind, when I had a complete mental break: Theo sat down in the booth in front of me.

I barely had time to register him, much less deal with the swarm of questions that erupted in my brain. Why was he here? What was he doing wearing a coat and tie, his hair slicked back so handsomely? Had Kallie seen him? *Would* Kallie see him? What might happen if she *did* see him? The world tilted on its side.

Theo spoke in a rush, as though he were trying to get all the words out on a deadline. "Hey. My family's here celebrating before the meet tomorrow, and I wanted to say hi."

"Hi," I said, none-too-brilliantly.

"Hi," he returned. His eyes scanned the room and he looked over his shoulder. I knew what he was watching for, and he knew I knew. For such a seemingly nice guy, why did Theo keep putting me in such awkward positions?

"I'm here with Kallie. We're having dessert," I said, almost defensively.

He nodded, as if he knew. "So, everything's… good?" That was a weird question. He looked at me probingly, as if expecting me to say something important. I had a sudden flash of when I'd shown Coach Corcoran my bruises by the pool; as he'd examined them, I'd realized Theo was standing not too far off, looking at them, too. He'd turned away from me, but not before I saw the question marks in his eyes. After practice I'd dressed in a hurry, announcing to the team at large that I was late for dinner plans, and bolting before Theo was out of the showers.

All of this went through my brain like a bullet, and I realized I'd need to choose my next few words very, very carefully. "Yeah, fine."

"Bike accident," he said, his voice filling with empathy. "That sucks."

"Yeah," I said, trying not to panic and trying not to look outside the dining room. It was barely a one-minute walk to the restrooms. If Kallie was in there for less than three minutes, things could shortly get very hairy.

"Look, Shan," Theo said, leaning in. He was very close to my face, and with the flickering candlelight in the booth, it suddenly felt weirdly intimate, like that time he'd touched me in the shower. He probably meant nothing by such gestures, but they made me feel odd.

He continued: "If you ever want to talk about anything, you know, and you don't feel comfortable talking to Coach C about it…"

"Why wouldn't I want to talk to Coach Corcoran?" I asked, my voice going sandpapery. Theo lifted an eyebrow and lowered his head a little: his expression said, "Do you really think I'm that dumb?"

"Look," I said, talking faster, really trying not to scan the doorway, "I'm fine. I know you have — had — some issues with the Corcorans…"

"Oh, is that what we're calling them? Issues?" Theo seemed somewhere between amused and irritated by this.

"We're having dessert," I said doggedly. "Seriously, it's fine. You should go."

"I'm not afraid of her," Theo said, looking into my eyes.

"You sure hightailed it today in front of the locker room."

"I don't want *you* in trouble," he said. For a split second, I thought he was going to reach for my hand. I nervously put them in my lap. My palms were so wet, my legs could feel them through my pants.

"I'm fine. I'll see you tomorrow."

"Not if I see you first," he said, scooting out of the booth. I'd never understood that expression, and it frankly just made me angrier considering I was already worked up. I had to drag my eyes away from him as he rejoined his family on the far side of the restaurant. As he sat back down, his back to the door, Kallie re-entered the restaurant and our server appeared with the bag. I fumbled getting my wallet out.

"Don't tell me they charged you for the dessert," Kallie said, disbelievingly. "You don't get an employee discount?"

"Discount, not free," I said, pulling out a few bills. My eyes unwillingly dragged themselves back to the table by the jazz combo: Theo and what looked like his mom, dad, and some siblings were laughing and enjoying their meal. They looked happy together. I thought of Zip's family and Shabbat dinner, and another dark wave of gloom settled over me. "And we need to tip."

"Yes, such excellent service," Kallie intoned dryly. "Well… Shall we?"

"We shall," I said, trying to sound forthright and commanding. As we moved towards the lobby, I put myself on the right and put my left arm around Kallie's waist, guiding her ever-so-slightly and blocking her view if she'd looked into the restaurant. All she probably would've seen was the back of Theo's head. Still, I figured better safe than sorry.

And then we were in the old-fashioned elevator with the wrought-metal door. When you went up you felt like you were in some ornate birdcage as you looked down on the Excelsior lobby and the lower hallways. I was holding the bag with the cheesecake, and Kallie was rubbing her hand over my butt. I was trying not to get too excited. She had the room key — an old-fashioned style key, with a little tag dangling off of it — already in her other hand, along with her shopping bag, and when she caught my eye she raised her eyebrows and smiled.

The Excelsior only had about twenty rooms, and as we stepped off the elevator at the top floor, and it was her turn to take my hand and guide me down the hallway, I had a sudden chill: what were the odds that she had she gotten the same room that my mom and I had stayed in once before, so many years ago?

She stopped at the end of the hall, in front of Room twenty-seven, and my heart clutched. The odds were too good.

Same door, though the staff had done a repair job on it to sand down the damage, and the splintered frame. They'd painted the hotel a couple years ago, so the door no longer showed any dark scuff marks or bruises from Frankie's late-night attack:

"I know you're in there, Fee!"

My mom and I cowering in the bathroom, door closed and locked, a suitcase propped uselessly against it. The cold, hard tile underneath us. The repeated THUD, THUD, THUD, WHAM! WHAM! WHAM! against the door. Frankie's voice yelling, yelling; my mom pulls me close, wraps her arms around my head. I feel the floor vibrating from Frankie's attack on the door to the room.

"FIONA!" It's barely even a voice; it's like an animal howling.

Doors are opening and closing; other voices shouting. Running footsteps. The sound of wood starting to crack and splinter under the assault. The door actually gives way and bursts open; Frankie's voice raging, a torrent of invective and threats.

"WHERE ARE YOU, you BITCH?"

Something heavy strikes the wall (a crowbar, we later find out; that's also what did the job on the door). Frankie is lashing out; the wall will need to be re-plastered, the flower-vase picture on the wall re-framed with new glass. Just as the door handle to the bathroom is rattling, and I'm pressed into my mom so tight, so tight, because there are boogeymen in the world and they will come to get you and one is outside and will kill my mother and eat me alive and I'm scared so scared so scared so scared…

The sound of yelling, and feet. Many feet. "POLICE! DROP YOUR WEAPON!" a voice yells. More crashes, heavy sounds. Frankie is yelling, is choking, is incoherent with rage. Screaming. Screaming. The room is being destroyed. Every employee in the hotel over two hundred pounds, plus two cops, has been deployed to wrestle Frankie to the ground, to grab the crowbar, to pull the forty-five out of Frankie's waistband, to cut the cuffs on those tattooed wrists with a "click" sound. The sound of wailing and cursing as Frankie is dragged away down the hall.

Handcuffs. Jesus. No wonder I freaked out when Kallie used them on me. Oh God. Oh God.

Kallie had opened the door, and turned to look at me. Without realizing it, I had my head in my hands, palms pressed against my temples to blot out the roaring in my ears. My eyes were shut tight, and I couldn't breathe. I was hyperventilating, and tears were running down my face. My lungs sounded like an accordion that had been thrown down a staircase.

"Shan," Kallie said, reaching for my forearm. She gripped ahold of it, and with one finger stroked the inside of my wrist. I completely lost it, starting to snuffle and bawl. She somehow got me inside the room, turned on a light, laid me down on the antique-style bed. I laid there, helpless as an infant, as she threw a piece of lingerie over the lampshade so the lighting became even dimmer, kicked off her shoes, and pulled off mine. She didn't talk, but her expression was concerned, as if she'd encountered something she didn't understand and was trying to figure out how to handle.

The room was pretty much just as I'd remembered it, though they had done some repairs to the broken picture, the scratched wall, the smashed chair. Still, it was remarkable how little had changed. My mom and I had lived in this room for almost two months after she'd left Frankie, once the threatening phone calls started. She'd gotten this job, and the manager, Mr Appleby, had let us take this room "off the books" because it ostensibly had plumbing problems. (I never saw any during the almost eight weeks we were there.) After Frankie went to jail, we moved to our current house. My mom still sends Christmas cards to the Appleby family, and spoke at his memorial service last year. Heart attack at forty-five: always happened to the nice ones.

Kallie lay down on the bed next to me, carefully wiping the side of my face where the tears had slid down towards my ears and onto the bedspread. She slowly ran her hands over my torso and neck, watching my face intently. She didn't talk, didn't hum or sing like my mom did when I had nightmares; she just breathed very carefully, as if trying to keep the noise to a minimum. After a while, I stopped crying and shaking and just lay very still.

She finally spoke. "Was it in this room that it happened?"

There was no way she could've known, but it sounded like she did. "Yes."

"Jail time?"

"Five years," I said. "How did you know?"

"I did some research this week," she said, looking at the wall where the new picture was hanging. "It took a while, but once I knew your mom's name, I cross-referenced a few things. It was big on the local news."

Yes. Yes, it was.

"You're such a nice boy," she went on, talking out loud as though she were verbalizing her thought processes. "I would've protected you, if I'd known you then."

"Would you?" I looked at her face, dim in the light of the room. I tried to imagine all that passion, all that fury I'd seen glimpses of this week, directed at someone trying to hurt me.

The problem was, she'd been the person this past week who'd hurt me.

"Yes," she said, sounding almost surprised that I'd doubted her. "You don't think I'd protect you from bad people?"

"I—"

"Shan, that's what I *want* to do." She rearranged herself on the bed, and pulled me close, holding me pietà-style, across her lap. She moved her hand inside my shirt, ran it over the bare skin, down to my stomach. My penis involuntarily began to stir. She breathed in my ear: "I want to help you get over this."

And then she was humming, not entirely on key, but gently; a song that took me a minute to recognize. It was Death Cab for Cutie's 'I Will Possess Your Heart.' And between the soft, humming notes, there were kisses. Kisses that seemed to take a bit of the hurt away. Kisses that made me forget about the bad stuff.

I wanted to resist her attentions, to say that I wasn't a baby, I wasn't a child, I wasn't helpless and I didn't need taking care of. But by the time she had my clothes off, and she'd slipped on the lingerie that was formerly

hanging over the lampshade, I wasn't in shape to say
much of anything.

Chapter 18

The sun filtered through the white curtains, and I felt drained, as though I were a piece of fruit that'd been juiced till only the pulp remained. I remembered the night before in flashes, a torrent of photographs that didn't quite cohere into a film.

What I remembered: the restaurant. Coming upstairs. An anxiety attack. Kallie holding me. Kallie soothing me. Kallie undressing me. Kallie…

I couldn't move my hands.

I propped my head up and looked left to right. Silk scarves were wrapped around my wrists, and securely tied to the bedposts. I was unclothed, splayed out on the bed, my hands tied to the posts, and the clock on the nightstand next to me said six thirty-five.

And I was supposed to be at school warming up for my first swim meet in less than an hour.

Kallie was nowhere in the room, and the bathroom door was wide open. On the large mirror over the desk, written in lipstick, was a scrawl the color of Kallie's lips: FACE YOUR FEARS.

Oh crap oh crap oh crap oh crap *oh crap.*

I remembered, at one point during the night, her reaching into her purse, and me saying, "Please, no handcuffs," and her murmuring, "Don't worry, I'll be gentle." And two beautiful silk scarves appeared out of the purse; scarves that were gently draped and dragged softly all over my body, as if they were wiping away the past, scarves that tied my hands together above my head and behind me, but loosely, as she straddled me and gave me That Smile, and said, "Now, isn't that nice?" And it was.

Now, however, the scarves, and my wrists, were at opposite ends of the bedposts, and secure. Very secure. She'd made sure of that.

I could yell, I thought. Yell for help. But then someone was sure to notify the manager and the staff, and them finding me naked and tied to a bed in one of their rooms was sure to backfire on my mom. Potentially getting her fired was a non-starter.

The room phone on the desk rang, five times. *Shit!* I pulled harder at the scarves, feeling them burn against my flesh from the friction. Hopeless. I kicked my legs, thrashed my body; nothing worked. I tried bumping the bed against the wall, then remembered that this was a corner room. There was nothing on the other side.

What was I going to do? What was I going to *do?*

My phone buzzed from across the room, where it was still lodged comfortably in my pocket. Fat lot of good that did right now! Someone, clearly was trying to get ahold of me. Kallie, to gloat a little at the predicament she'd put me in? *I'll help you get over this,* she'd said. Was this her bizarre idea of therapy? Or just another power move, reminding me she was always, always in charge? Yes, I thought, my mind slowly defrosting: that was exactly what she did. She broke me down, made me vulnerable, so that I was dependent on her, wanted her, needed her. Then she was in control again.

What if it was my mom, in case she hadn't read my text last night saying I was staying overnight with a friend (insert bitter laughter)?

No one knows I'm here, I thought, in a cold sweat of panic. Zip and Sonya knew I was coming here for dessert, but no one knew I was staying here.

Wait! One person might.

Knock knock. It was polite knocking; the kind you did when you weren't sure someone was awake. The voice, muffled, cautious and almost fearful, but distinct. "Shan?"

Theo!

"Theo!" I yelled/whispered, trying to be loud enough so he could hear me, but not loud enough that it'd cause a disturbance.

"Shan, what's going on?" Rattling of the door, thumping, banging. *(Thumping at the door, again. Do not panic. Do not panic. DO NOT PANIC.)* "It's me, Theo! Can you open the door?"

"No!" I cried. I was almost sobbing with helplessness, with relief, with embarrassment. "I can't get out of bed. I'm stuck! Do you have a key?"

Theo swore, and I heard more rattling. I thrashed my body again, still straining at the scarves. The last thing I wanted was for Theo to see me like this!

"Shan, I'm trying to use my pocketknife to get the lock," Theo said in low, urgent tones. "I'm going to need to use a Starbucks card, as well. This may take a sec. I'm trying to do it while no one's in the hallway."

"You don't have a key?" I asked again. Duh, of course he didn't; otherwise, he would've been in the room by now.

"No, the front desk wouldn't give me one," he said. More scrabbling noises and scraping. The door to this room is just cursed, I thought grimly.

"Good thing this is a vintage hotel," Theo muttered. "Modern key cards would never work like this. And… gotcha!"

With a CLICK, the lock slid out of its slot, the door opened, and a not-very-awake-looking Theo burst into the room, pushing the door closed behind him. He had on a T-shirt that looked like it had been grabbed off of his bedroom floor, and his hair was a mess. But based on the way his eyes widened and his jaw went slack, I could only imagine what I looked like.

"Jesus, Shan," Theo said, his voice dropping to a rasp.

"Untie me!" I said, indicating my wrists. He was at the bed in two strides, working on the knots. One came off easily; for the other, after he struggled with it for a second, he whipped out the pocketknife and sliced through.

"How'd you know I was here?" I choked, rubbing my aching wrist.

"Sonya," Theo said, grabbing my clothes and tossing them at me. "Hurry, we can talk while you're dressing. I'm parked downstairs. Maybe we can still make it to school by seven thirty."

"You're a lifesaver," I sighed, throwing on my clothes. I was in "go" mode now. I didn't even have time to feel mortified about how he'd found me. Obviously, it's one thing to see someone naked in a locker room or a gym shower; it's another to find them tied to a four-poster bed.

"What did Sonya do?" I asked, yanking on my shirt and sweater in one move. My phone was buzzing again I ignored it.

"She texted me yesterday," Theo said, looking at me very intently, "and asked what I was doing last night. Nothing, I said, except I was supposed to have dinner with my family before today's meet. So she asked me if there was any way I could ask my family to have dinner at Catch, or come by later in the evening, and make sure you were okay."

Son of a bitch. That explained last night. No wonder Sonya had let me go so easily, knowing Theo was going to check on me later.

"But you didn't seem okay when I saw you," Theo went on, words rushing together. "So I decided to swing by here this morning on the way to school, and see if you were still here. It's only a five-minute detour. And just as I'm walking into the lobby, guess who I see walking out?"

"Kallie," I said, knowing full well.

He didn't even have to nod. His words came in a rush. "I tried calling your phone, but you didn't answer. The front-desk clerk was weird about telling me where you were, so they called up here, but still no answer." He raised his eyebrows, indicating the shreds of scarf. "I tried to explain that I was supposed to pick you up at the room, and I knew your name, but they were still reluctant." He grinned. "Then the desk clerk rehung the key someone had checked in, and I figured the odds were pretty good it was the one Kallie had just left. So I ran up here. Worst case, I could've run around to all the rooms calling your name."

"You're a prince," I said, grabbing the last of my stuff.

"Do we need to swing by home and get your swim stuff?"

"It's all in my locker at school. We can go straight there."

"Not without breakfast," he said, frowning at me. "Didn't you learn *anything* at your other school's swimming competitions? We'll drive-through and grab an egg-white English muffin sandwich and some fruit at McDonald's. Our heat doesn't start till nine; that'll give us some time to digest. I've got protein bars and bananas in my backpack for later."

It was one of those moments where you just can't believe how good people can be. I put up my hand to do that 'bro-shake' thing, but then found myself pulling him in for a real hug, and he put both arms around me for a moment. He rested his head on my shoulder, and I smelled sweat, and Tide laundry detergent, and sleep. It was a good smell.

Then he saw the mirror and said, "What's THAT?"

"A message for me, apparently," I said through clenched teeth. My phone buzzed again. It had to be Sonya or Zip.

"Some message," Theo growled. "You haven't looked at your phone yet, have you?"

"No," I said, as we left the room and started down the hallway.

"Well, I don't know what she's referencing," Theo said grimly, as we entered the elevator, "but stuff's been racing across Instagram like crazy the past couple hours."

Instagram?

The elevator started its descent, as Theo handed me his phone. He'd already opened up the application, and he looked almost sad as I glanced at what was posted on it, leaving my stomach back up on the top floor as the little cage sank down, down.

It was me.

It was me in the hotel room, asleep.

It was me, asleep, my hands tie to the bedposts. And absolutely, full-on naked.

Oh Jesus God.

"Shan!"

Theo and I barely had the elevator gate open, and Boris was already waving us over to the desk. Boris was one of the assistant managers: a big, gloomy, bearded Russian guy who always looked like he might burst into tears at any moment.

Cursing under my breath, and with a lightning-quick glance at Theo, I ran to the desk. "What's up, Boris?"

"Oh, Meester Shan," Boris wheezed, hands fluttering, looking like he had to tell me the Soviet Union had collapsed all over again. I didn't have time for this.

"*What,* Boris?"

"The lady," Boris harrumphed uncomfortably, gesturing out the front door and towards the world. "She turn in key. She says, you pay for room when you leave, *da?*"

My stomach was already churning like a washer full of throw rugs. Now, it seemed to explode in a sea of foam and goo. "She… said what?"

"The room," Boris said, wiping his forehead, breaking into a sweat with embarrassment. "She got room for you both last night, but she say you pay when you leave. We figure, since your mother work here, we bend rules, but hotel was very full last night. You pay cash?"

I. Am. Going. To. Kill. Her.

"No, not cash," I said, trying to get my mind to kick into high gear. "I, um—"

"I'm paying," Theo said, out of left field. He pulled out his wallet. "How much?"

"Oh well," Boris said, his eyes suddenly lighting up at the sight of Theo's billfold stuffed with bills and credit cards. "Mr Shan gets employee discount, but if he's not paying—"

"Boris," I said, trying not to grit my teeth lest they shatter, "you're not charging me for the full room price, are you?" It was a difference of almost a hundred and fifty dollars.

"It was for he and the lady's anniversary," Theo said smoothly, holding up a VISA card. "So, it *was* for him. The employee rate is. . ?"

"Eighty dollars," Boris said, slumping a little in defeat.

"Great," Theo said, smiling. "And we're kind of in a hurry, so if you could…"

Boris lumbered off to run the credit card. I turned to Theo to thank him, but when he looked at me his face had gone cold and hard.

"Sorry," I muttered.

He waved his hand and looked even more nettled.

"You didn't have to do that," I said. Theo looked down at the floor, propping his arms on the counter, his blond hair falling past his face.

I continued, trying not to sound snappish. "I'll get breakfast, and I'll pay you back—"

"Shan," he said, snapping to attention, frustration flooding his face. "It's not about the money."

I didn't say anything. Now it was my turn to look at the floor. My face flushed crimson. I could feel it.

"You know," he said, his eyes boring into me. "I know. We've both been there. You've got to get out."

"I know," I said softly. It was the conversation with Sonya all over again.

"It's only beginning," he continued, as Boris handed him the receipt and he signed it in a blur. "Right now? This is only the start. What else has happened? She's hit you, right? That's where the bruises came from."

I grabbed his arm and pulled him out through the lobby, away from anyone who might hear, but he was wise to me. "Oh, you don't want anyone to hear, is that it? Like your mom's co-workers? Who else have you been lying to?"

"No one!" I said, trying not to cry. He was walking really fast and it was hard to keep up.

"I'll bet," he said acidly. He was at his car, an older red Toyota Camry, in a few strides. He pulled the door open for me to throw my stuff in, then turned and almost glared at me. "How much do Sonya and Zip know?"

"They know the basics," I mumbled.

"Well, they're about to know a lot more," he said, slamming the back door shut and opening the front door. "That Instagram picture will spread like wildfire. And I'll bet you she's got a lot more."

My heart jumped and twisted in my chest. That didn't even occur to me. I stood by the open car door, almost shaking.

"Are you gonna get in?" Theo finally said, his voice softening. He looked at me with a pitying expression. I somehow folded myself into the front seat, and he turned on the ignition. A blast of Beyonce's "Crazy In Love" from the stereo nearly deafened me. We exchanged sad glances as he shut the radio off.

A few blocks away, he finally spoke. "Hey, I'm sorry I yelled."

"Don't be," I said, my eyes finally filling with tears. I looked out the window away from him, but I felt his touch on my shoulder. I let the tears run down my face without wiping them away. His voice was as soft and gentle as a baby's blanket. "It's not your fault."

"It's not?" I could barely get out those two sentences without sobbing.

"No," he said, shaking his head. "I've been there, remember? I've met the family. I know how they can mess with your mind. I know the pressure we're both under. I may not be on a swimming scholarship, but I know the pressure."

"I can't think when I'm around her," I said, staring out the window at the gray and green world. "She just—overpowers me."

"I know," Theo sighed. "Eddie's the same way. He came on really strong, really charming. He made me laugh, made me feel special and kind of daring. Excited. The bad boy attitude. The sex was incredible. Then the control thing started: Where you going? Who're you talking to? Why didn't you check in with me?" He shook his head, remembering.

I was thunderstruck. Kallie and Eddie had the same *modus operandi*. I wonder if they even realized it.

"And then," he continued, grimacing a little at the memory, "his temper started spiraling. Eddie never hit me, but he broke things: a door, my car window, a phone he threw at a wall."

"Do you think it's the steroids, from all the lifting he's doing?" I queried. That would explain a lot.

"Maybe," Theo said. "Maybe a propensity for bad tempers runs in the family, and that's just pouring more gas on the fire." He raised an eyebrow and gave me a significant look. "After all, Kallie doesn't do steroids." He had me there.

We drove through McDonald's, getting our egg-white sandwiches and fruit. Nothing fried. Fortunately, I'd eaten like a king at Zip's last night, so I wasn't that hungry this morning. It was more about keeping the metabolism revved and idling, so you have something in reserve when you need it during a race. Theo also gave me an extra protein bar.

"I just don't know what to do," I said, once we were back on the road and heading towards school. "I mean, the swim team is my ticket right now. It might make the difference between college, and not. And if I break up with Kallie, I'm not sure…" I let the sentence hang there for a minute, as the world whizzed by in a blur of watercolors. "I don't know if her uncle would give me the same sorts of opportunities."

"Shan-man," Theo said. No one had ever called me this before, and it made me feel good. He grinned at me, and I saw the overgrown Tom Sawyer again. "You've got to stop undercutting yourself. Grow a sack, and admit that you're good."

"Good?"

"A good swimmer," he said, punching/tickling me in the stomach and making me giggle. "A good guy. Jesus, have you no self-esteem at all? Or do you do these mind games to *make* people give you compliments?"

"Like what?"

"Oh, here we go," he said, laughing. "Okay, fine. You're a star swimmer; you seem like a good student; you're a loyal boyfriend who takes *no* end of crap from a psychotic bitch…"

I was really giggling now.

"You seem like a great friend, if Zip and Sonya are to be believed," Theo continued, looking speculatively.

"Good son, loves his mama, wants to make her proud. Oh yeah — and definitely easy on the eyes."

"Oh, you noticed," I said, trying to sound casual.

"Darn right I noticed. Those eyes? That mop-top of hair? That tight bod? Phew." He exhaled, and wiggled his eyebrows again. "You played for my team, I'd be all over you. But I know you're all about the psychotic *bee-yotches,* so…" He pulled into a parking spot, and added as an afterthought, "Not that I don't have a track record with the damaged and crazy…"

We were both bent over to grab our bags of food at my feet, and it was when he was coming back up that our faces were right next to each other, and I smelled that sleepy, unshowered smell again, and without even thinking about it, before I even knew what was happening, I leaned in and kissed him, gently, on the lips.

The universe imploded.

Theo pulled away, staring at me, his face contorted with shock.

"You're just… so nice," I said, my throat suddenly parched. "I mean… you're such a good friend. Thank you."

"Friends don't usually kiss each other," Theo said, very slowly, staring at me. His eyes were huge and very blue. They shimmered momentarily.

"I know," I said. The words all came out at once. "You just came and rescued me, and you helped me, and you're kind, and you're just…"

Now, I was at a loss for words. I tried again. "You're just…"

"Don't kiss me again," Theo said slowly and carefully.

"I'm sorry, I won't—"

"Unless you *mean* it."

The words dangled in the air. We sat and looked at each other, in the front seat of a car, on a gray Saturday morning in a near-empty school parking lot. Two boys, wondering if they should kiss each other again, and what it might mean if they did.

Finally, Theo spoke. "We'd better go in."

"Yeah."

We didn't speak on the walk to the gym, or while changing at opposite ends of the locker room as other swim-team guys started trickling in, whooping and hollering and excited for the day. We didn't look at each other, either, over the next hour as we helped drag the equipment out, and the team started warming up, and the scoreboard was turned on, and they let the spectators in. From my vantage point, bobbing in the water, I saw Kallie enter from outside, wearing a striped sundress and a broad-brimmed sunhat. She marched straight towards the spectator stands as though leading a parade. Which, as it turns out, she was.

Behind her, in a black T-shirt and jeans, came Eddie.

Behind him, all laughing and talking together, came my mother, Sonya, and Zip.

Now, I was in the deep end of the pool, for certain.

Chapter 19

"Swimmers, take your mark!"

It was the start of the hundred-meter freestyle, my best event. I stood exposed on the diving board, looking down at the water, only a Speedo, cap, and goggles to protect me from the world. My bruises didn't look as bad as they did yesterday morning. Still, I was hyper-aware of them, and the endless comments and "Whoas!" from various swim team members hadn't helped. *I fell off my bike, no big deal, seriously, I'm fine…*

I was afraid to look to my right, but I knew Theo was there, also readying himself. We were among the fastest guys on the team, so we were both assigned to the middle lanes of the pool. I'd snuck a couple peeks at him during the earlier events, but he steadfastly refused to look at me, keeping his jaw tight and his eyes locked dead ahead.

I tried not to look up in the stands, either, though I'd done a couple lightning-quick glances earlier in that direction. Kallie sat, regally imperious, the Dowager Empress surveying the Forbidden City's eunuchs. She had on black sunglasses for some reason, even though we were indoors, and the light coming through the windows wasn't excessively bright. *Did she not want me to see her eyes?* I wondered. Quite possibly. Her hands were locked together tightly, as though each of them was in a life-or-death struggle with the other.

Eddie looked even grimmer than she did, and his T-shirt looked like it might rip off of his torso at any moment. His huge, thick neck swiveled as he watched the swimmers warming up, back and forth and up and down the length of the pool, as though it was too difficult for him to just move his eyes.

Why would he be here? I wondered. Then I remembered their uncle was my coach; maybe they were there to support him. Then I realized another potential motivation: Theo. Eddie wanted to see Theo swim. Or *maybe,* I thought, sneaking another quick look at Kallie's impassive face, they were banking on Eddie's being there to make Theo so rattled, he'd blow his events. I wasn't sure about Eddie's motives, but I wouldn't have put that past Kallie. After the hotel and the Instagram thing, I could only begin to imagine what she was capable of.

My mom was sitting a couple rows up from the Corcorans with Zip and Sonya, who were animatedly chatting with her and pointing out various guys from the team. My mom was laughing and smiling and looked like she was still in college, with her hair down and loose, and her expensive leather jacket from Nordstrom's. Zip was keeping up a running dialogue about who knew what, and of course they all had bagel sandwiches with them. I'd had breakfast, but I would've killed for one of those sandwiches right then—not just because it would've tasted good, but to have been sitting on the bleachers surrounded by people I cared about.

I looked at the other end of the pool. It seemed very far away, like one of those nightmares where you're trying to get away from something and the hallway you're running down keeps elongating and stretching further and further. Just five days earlier, I'd been the new *wunderkind* of the team; now, just trying to move my muscles through the water—including my still-tender wrists—seemed like it was going to take ever shred of effort I had.

Just get through this, I said to myself. You know how to do this. You can do this. You can talk to Kallie later. Now, just—

SCREECH!!

The blast of the horn sounds, and I'm airborne, then knifing into the water. After being out of it for the past several minutes, being back in it is like returning to my home environment. I draw strength from it, like Aquaman, feel the rush of it past my body. I'm a flying fish, I'm a fired torpedo, I'm a bullet train whizzing into the Chunnel from England to Paris. I see the end wall coming at me and flip over, then zoom forward, free again, no obstacles. My arms churn, my legs kick, my head swivels. Far away, I hear the sound of cheering obscured by splashing and bubbles as my face moves in and out of the water. Do I hear my name being yelled? Maybe.

My adrenaline is surging. I think of Kallie, of Eddie, of Frankie, and I don't feel weak or frightened, I feel enraged. A crackle of energy electrifies my limbs; my strokes are even more powerful, the giant sweeping movements of something prehistoric in a primeval lagoon. I don't feel any fear, I feel hatred. And the hatred energizes and empowers me. I swim like I've never swum in my life.

There was a storm of bubbles, and then my hand scraped against the wall. I reared out of the water like a killer whale, jumping and turning, as the stands erupted into screams. In the distance, I saw the scoreboard: fifty-five seconds. I'd sliced ten seconds off my best time.

Everyone was going nuts in the stands. My mom had only met Zip and Sonya twice before, but she was hugging them and crying. Zip was jumping up and down like a crazy person, and Sonya had her hands clasped as if in prayer, her face covered by a gigantic smile. Two rows down, Kallie and Eddie were also up and applauding, but with an odd sort of reluctance. Then I realized Theo was jumping up and down with me, and grabbing me, and laughing like a crazy man: he'd shaved eight seconds off of his best time, and come in second, right behind me. Then we were both jumping around and laughing and hugging like fools.

We both got out of the water and milled around with our teammates as everyone got their scores. In the stands, Kallie was actually glowering down at me, as I looked up at her, my arm still wrapped around Theo's shoulders. I gave her and Eddie, whose eyes looked like they were about to bug out of his head, a big, wet, cheerful wave. My mom, Sonya and Zip were all waving their arms off at us.

We still had more events to get through over the next few hours—I was still signed up for a 500-meter solo and a relay—but this was the big one: I'd broken through. I wasn't afraid of anything any more. Nothing else that happened today could take away this glow, I was 100% certain.

Not even breaking up with Kallie.

***

"My *star!*" my mom cried, running towards me, Zip and Sonya right behind her. I should've felt more embarrassed, I guess, but at that moment, coming out of the locker room with my hair still damp and smelling of chlorine, getting pulled into my mom's embrace was all I could ask for. She was crying again, and her cheeks felt wet against mine and on my T-shirt as she breathed, "Oh, I was *so* proud of you! You did so good. *So* good!"

"You rocked it out, Shan," Sonya said, hugging me too. Zip was busy hugging Theo. I had no idea if they even knew each other, but they were both bouncing around like those little rubber balls you're never supposed to give to little kids lest they break everything in the house.

207

I felt warm, accomplished, exhausted, grateful, loved; I felt like I'd been to the top of Mount Olympus. Not only had I broken my personal record on the freestyle, I'd placed second in the hundred-meter relay. I was having one hell of a good day.

"Great job, Shan."

The voice was simultaneously sharp yet dull, like a razor that would cut your throat, but not swiftly: more like in jagged, tearing motions. Kallie stood behind everyone, Eddie a few paces behind her, watching all of us as though she were waiting for some sort of invitation to join in. I wasn't about to do that.

"Thanks," I said, shortly. I made brief eye contact with Eddie, then turned away, getting swept into a big hug from Zip. As I was looking away, she tried again. "So, you broke a record."

"Yeah," I said curtly. Sonya, Zip, Theo and my mom all stopped jumping around and suddenly seemed to become aware of the conversation. My mom was looking at me with a thousand questions in her eyes, but I wasn't in the mood for introductions and small talk.

"So, you faced your fears," Kallie said, just a hint of smugness in her voice. She seemed to be actually daring me to reveal the events of the morning prior to the meet. I wasn't about to give her the satisfaction: it might have embarrassed her. But having no reaction at all, I knew, would mortally wound her. And right now, I was all about the sword going in deep.

"Guess so," I said flatly. There was a really awkward pause, like people were waiting for me to do or say something more decisive and give them their cues in this scene. I wasn't feeling very generous.

"Aren't you going to introduce me to your mom?" Kallie said, a threat lurking behind the words. Her eyes were flashing. Behind her, Eddie looked at the ground, possibly to avoid the brewing confrontation; possibly because he didn't want to look at Theo.

"No," I said, so loudly and so harshly, it shocked even me. Sonya's eyes widened and she tried very hard to mask an amused smile. Unfortunately, Kallie caught sight of it, and her face hardened into a death mask. Behind me, I felt Zip and Theo press in a little closer to my back and shoulders, as if forming a phalanx.

"Shannon Peter," my mother said, her face falling and her voice taking on the stern/disappointed tone that used to infallibly bring tears to my eyes. At this moment, however, I was so mad at Kallie — and now mad at my mom for using my middle name in front of everyone, as though I were a child — that I felt myself turning red with anger.

"Okay," I said roughly, raising my voice and shrugging off Sonya, Zip, and Theo's gentle hands. "An introduction? Mom, this is Kallie, my *ex*—" (I made sure to almost spit the word) "—girlfriend. Happy?"

"Oh, is *that* how you're going to play it," Kallie said. She looked almost pleased at the drama erupting.

"Yeah, that's how I'm rolling," I almost-snarled at her. At that moment, I wanted to grab her and shake her till her teeth rattled, anything to get that smirk off her face. "You're lucky I don't press charges against you for that picture, let alone everything else you did to me last night."

"*That* picture?" She was openly amused now; maybe, based on her slightly breathless tone, even turned on. "You think there's only *one?*"

That froze me in my tracks. Of course there was more than one. Of course. She'd keep them in reserve, and would keep using them as long as she wanted.

"Picture?" Zip asked, bewildered. I looked briefly at him, Sonya, and my mom's confused faces. Thanks to losing my cool, I'd just 'outed' myself. *Shit.* I stood there, flummoxed and red-faced, as everyone stared at each other.

"How's our merman?" boomed Coach Corcoran, suddenly, in the middle of all of us and clapping his hand on my shoulder. (Why did everyone keep *touching* me right now?) "Did you all see the great show?"

"Great show," Kallie echoed, eyes boring into me like lances. "Shan was telling us about how much *attention* he's going to be getting in the near future."

"Kallie…" Eddie actually put his hand on her arm. She shrugged it off. We were like duelists in a field, weapons cocked and pointed, ignoring the support of our worried seconds.

"Shan, let's go," Theo said, unintentionally mimicking Eddie's gesture and touching my arm. I saw Eddie's face go rigid, and Kallie's eyes widened.

"Don't you touch him," Kallie (or was it Eddie?) snarled, and suddenly both younger Corcorans were heading towards me. Sonya moved to block them, and their uncle actually had to step in between all of us.

"All right, all right… Let's simmer this down." He eyed Sonya and Zip balefully. "What are *you* doing here?"

"We're spectators," Sonya said, not backing down one iota but suddenly looking indescribably weary at having to explain herself.

"Why are you yelling at *her?*" I almost shouted, suddenly aware of how he'd singled out Sonya, of all people. I was sick of all of them, the entire Corcoran family. I was sick of pretending, I was sick of making nice, I was sick of the whole damn charade.

The coach gave me a look of wide-eyed surprise, then his eyes narrowed in a way I had never seen in the previous week. "Son, I think you'd better watch your tone."

"He's *my* son," my mom said, moving in amongst all my friends and snaking an arm around my shoulders. I forgot how mad I'd been at her a few seconds ago. All I wanted now was for her to protect me. "If you're going to be his coach, I'd expect you to make sure no harm comes to him. And it seems to me this girl may not be such a good influence."

"*I'm* not a good influence?" Kallie's voice was louder and harsher than ever. Several people around the pool turned and stared at us.

"Ask about the bike accident," Zip suddenly said, as everyone turned and stared at him. "Shan knows."

"Which one?" Sonya said bitterly. Everyone swiveled back and looked at her.

"There's more than one?" my mom looked at me, her face clouded in confusion.

I took a deep breath, feeling everyone's eyes on me. "There's only one," I said, very quietly. "I didn't fall off my bike — Zip did. Because someone tried to run him off the road." I looked right at Kallie, whose face didn't move but whose eyes flashed the message *I hate you I hate you I hate you* at me, like a traffic signal, over and over.

"And Shan didn't have a bike accident," Theo suddenly said, his hands yanking my shirt up so everyone could see my still-visible bruises sprayed across my torso. He looked at Kallie with obvious revulsion, as though she were a squashed tarantula. "*She hurt him.*"

I couldn't really describe the sound that came next.

It sounded partly like a cry, and partly like a wail. It sounded like someone dying inside. It would have been the most awful sound I'd ever heard, but I'd heard variations of it several times before in the past. It came from my mom's throat, and with a moan and a gush of tears, she slowly collapsed against Zip's comforting bulk. "No," she quietly keened in a voice that made my heart break into a thousand pieces. "No, no, no, no…"

Her legs gave way and she fell, like a falling star, in slow motion. I knelt, helped catch her as she went down. Zip eased her down and Theo assisted us. I was dimly aware of Coach Corcoran pushing his niece and nephew away, hissing at them as people stared at us. "What the hell is he talking about? What did you *do? What did you do?*"

***

In the end, we drove to Sonya's. Her house was closest, and her father, the doctor, was home. Her mother was visiting Sonya's aunt in Portland for the weekend.

"She'll be all right," Dr Larkin said, checking my mom's pulse one more time. "I don't think she needs to go to the hospital, but I think she'd be better off resting at home, once she wakes up. She definitely needs some fluids. Does she have to work this afternoon?"

"She has the day off," I said, from where I was kneeling by the couch, holding my mom's other hand. I don't know a lot of people who would've not batted an eye when four teenage kids and one semi-conscious woman showed up at their front door, but Dr Larkin just went with it. He was around six-foot-five, with skin the color of rosewood, and immaculately dressed for the golf course. He had delayed his tee time for half an hour to look at my mom, who seemed to be drifting in and

213

out of consciousness. Whenever she looked at me, she just started crying and closed her eyes again, and seemed to fall asleep.

Zip was sitting in the rocking chair, leaning forward, hands clasped. He was staring intently at both of us. The living room was the most gorgeous thing I'd ever seen. Every piece of furniture looked like it came from some sort of expensive catalog or had been handed down over the past couple millennia. Zip, in the midst of all this luxury, was a study in contrast.

But Dr Larkin didn't seem to care that Zip was wearing basketball shorts and ancient, torn sneakers in the living room, and he didn't seem to care that we stretched my mom out on the Chippendale sofa and that she was crying on their cushions. His eyes were kind, and his voice was smooth and gentle. "You all stay as long as you need. I'll be back in a few hours, if you want me to look at her again."

"Where's Sonya and Theo?" I asked Zip after Dr Larkin had left.

"Upstairs in Sonya's room," Zip said. "They're… debriefing."

"Why don't we just post the whole week on Facebook or Instagram," I said, somewhat bitterly. "Let's just let everyone know. The whole school, the town, everyone."

"Shan," Zip said, very gently. "You can be upset. It's okay. But we're not the bad guys."

"I know," I said, my face flushing with shame.

"It was going to happen sometime," Zip went on. "It couldn't stay underground forever. What if something really bad happened to you?"

"I think that was my mom's fear," I said, brushing her hair off her forehead. I had the strangest out-of-body moment: me, as a parent, and my mom as a child. Me taking care of her. Me.

There was nothing but a blank spot in my mind after that.

"So, now you know," Zip said. "Now you know what Kallie's capable of."

"That was while we were together," I said. "The problem now is, we're broken up. God only knows what that's going to bring."

"At least we're all on the same page," Zip said. I now realized he was holding a cup of tea in his hand. He carefully passed it to me so I could bring it to my mom's lips. At the smell and the feel of the porcelain against her lips, she took a sip or so, then seemed to fall asleep again as I set it down, trying not to rattle it and disturb her.

Zip yawned and stretched. "Heckuvva morning," he said, tapping his heels on the carpet. "What time is it, two? Gads, been up for hours." He rose, tiptoeing out of the room. "Let me holler upstairs for Sonya and ask about lunch." He went into the foyer and called up the stairs. "Sonya!"

"What?" came from upstairs, distantly.

"What in the fridge is okay to eat for lunch?" Zip yelled, noticing me frowning mightily at the noise. In the far distance outside, I heard the sound of tires squealing. Geez, wasn't there any quiet around here? My mom frowned in her sleep and murmured something.

"*What?* I can't hear you," Sonya yelled from upstairs, opening her bedroom door just enough to be audible. I heard Theo laughing, then more noise outside. Vrrooom, vroom, *screeeeech.*

"I *said*," Zip intoned, climbing the stairs, "what in the fridge—"

That's when the gunshots came, and the bullets smashed through the upstairs window of Sonya's room, facing the street. There was the sound of bodies hitting the floor, and then a scream.

I threw myself across my mom's body as she jerked wildly, thrashing, also screaming, screaming. I was dimly aware that the shots seemed directed upstairs, but didn't want to take the chance.

There were another couple shots, and more sounds of breaking glass, of tiny shards and particles exploding in the air. Tires screeched as the vehicle in the street drove away, and the house caught its breath in horrified silence for a few short moments, before the sirens began.

Chapter 20

Zip, on his way up the staircase, had hit the floor immediately. Despite his Playdough physique, years of gaming had given him the reflexes of a superhero. But Sonya had been standing near her window, the one facing the street, and thus received a barrage of scratches from the shattering glass, as well as burn across her shoulder.

The big question now: did the bullet go through Theo's arm, or his shoulder, and had it missed the bone? There was too much blood on his arm, shoulder, and chest, not to mention the upstairs walls and carpets of Sonya's room, to tell at this point, and he was too doped up to talk.

My mom had had to be sedated. My freak-out at The Excelsior the other night had only been a fraction of what she was going through. It had taken two good-sized ambulance drivers to restrain her enough to get her into the ambulance. She'd been unconscious for hours.

There were so many people in the waiting area, even though now it was late evening and visiting hours were ending soon. Zip's mom was sitting with Sonya's dad and holding his hand, while another doctor spoke to them in hushed tones. Sonya leaned against her father,

her beautiful face and neck sporting several large scratches. She'd been lucky no glass pieces had actually wedged themselves, like tiny killer icicles, into her flesh. She was staring at the ceiling light, as though waiting for it to call her home. Her father just looked grim.

Theo's mom and dad were sitting outside of surgery, also holding each other's hands. They were handsome and tan and athletic, just like him, but right now they both looked nauseous and exhausted. They kept craning their necks to look at the doors to the emergency room, wondering how their son was doing, their eyes tired and fearful.

The only one who seemed to have any energy at all was Zip. There was a news lady there, lurking at the end of the hallway with a sound guy and TV camera man, and the lady — Cheri Nightsong, one of those cheerful blonde "Doomsday is coming, but first! Casseroles you can freeze!" types — was pumping him for questions about the drive-by. Zip, as the only witness who hadn't been shot, upstairs at Sonya's, was handling the interview, modestly deflecting his caring for Sonya and Theo until the paramedics showed up. ("Scout training," Zip said cheerfully, as the reporter chick stared at him blankly.)

So far, there hadn't been an arrest — that I knew of — but I'd watched enough *Law and Order* in my life to know that most crimes were a matter of motive plus opportunity. I could think of only one person who hated all of us enough, and who had access to a gun safe in the house, to do this.

As if she could read my mind, the news lady said to Zip, "Do you have any ideas as to who would do such a thing?"

Zip paused, then shook his head carefully. "No one should do such a thing, period." The news lady nodded solemnly; they had their final shot and quote for the story. Tragic, just tragic, and no, as Cheri Nightsong put it, thank goodness there were no drugs or gangs ("that we're aware of at this time") involved in this incident. (If Sonya ever heard the casual racism implicit in that line, she would hunt that reporter down and skin her alive.)

"Shan?"

I turned and looked in the dimly lit room, with the stars hanging outside the window in the black night sky like they were on a child's mobile. My mom was almost in silhouette with the lights turned down as far as they were, but I could tell her head was turned towards me.

I went in and sat in the chair next to her, taking her hand, as I thought about our stupid fight from a couple days prior. My eyes blurred as I stroked her fingers. Who else did I have in my life that loved me this much?

"Hi baby," Mom whispered. I *was* crying now; she hadn't called me that for a while. I put her hand against my face and lowered my head, and just let the tears come. She reached out with her other hand and stroked my hair.

Eventually, she whispered, "Why are you crying?"

"Because I was scared for you," I said, trying not to break into hiccupping sobs. "I didn't know what happened to you at the pool, and then at Sonya's…"

"Sonya's. . ?" My mom looked quizzical. She doesn't even remember, I thought.

"We went there after the swim meet, after you fainted. Her dad took care of you."

"Oh." She frowned a little, worriedly. Her eyes still looked anxious. "Then what?"

I wondered how to put it into words, so I spoke slowly, as though putting a jigsaw puzzle together, piece by piece. "Then… there was a drive-by. Someone shot upstairs, and Sonya and Theo got hurt." Her face registered shock and concern. "But it's okay now," I added hurriedly. "We got here, and Theo's in surgery, and Sonya just got a little scraped up from some glass. It'll be okay," I repeated, trying to believe it.

My mom gestured for some water; I gave her a sip. She swallowed, and struggled to pull herself up a little bit. I rearranged the pillow for her, so she wasn't lying down. I wondered if she'd hold my hand again, but she didn't reach for it. Instead, she looked straight ahead at the blank wall, and said, very slowly, "No, Shan. This is not okay."

"But it is," I went on doggedly. "Theo's wound wasn't life-threatening; he just needs to be patched up. And—"

"Shan," my mom said, turning her head and looking right into my eyes. "Did that girl really hurt you, like Theo said?"

You wouldn't think it was so hard to say the smallest, simplest word, but I had to dig into the pit of my stomach to find my last ounce of strength to say it, and my voice still wavered. "Yes."

My mom nodded slowly, and tears began to come to her eyes again; this time, however, her face didn't crumple and she didn't sob. She just looked at me, searching my face for something she couldn't find. "This is all my fault," she murmured, brokenly.

"It's not," I said, too hurriedly. I knew it sounded like it was.

"Yes, it is," she said wearily. "I should've done a better job protecting you. All those years…"

"Mom—"

"All those years," she said again, shaking her head, letting the tears fall. "I knew we should've left sooner. And that last night at The Excelsior… I should've had you in therapy after that."

"Did you know that Kallie and I were in that exact same room Friday?" A bit more information than I meant to reveal, but I was caught up in the moment.

My mom looked at me in shock. "Oh, Shan, *no*," she half-moaned. "What were you doing there?"

It was bad enough, I decided to eliminate a few details. "We spent the night," I said, the words coming in a rush. "It was supposed to be a romantic night. But…"

"Did she get that room on *purpose?*" my mom asked, looking at me perturbed. I was thunderstruck. There was no way Kallie could know that, could she? Yet she'd said something about checking me out over the past week. Despite my name being kept out of the media at the time, she could've cross-referenced Frankie and my mom's names, and if she dug enough she could've found the articles. Hell, she could've even found the original news clips. Then, when she went to the bathroom Friday night, all she had to do was stop by the front desk while I'd been busy with Theo, slip someone a bill as incentive for some information…

"I don't know," I said honestly. "I hope she wouldn't."

"Shan," my mom said, taking my hand again. "I'm so sorry I pushed you to get closer to that family. I didn't… I thought…"

"It's okay," I said, rubbing my hand over her fingers, feeling the wear and tear on them from years of work. "They seemed nice — at first. Kallie seemed nice. Then it… changed."

"When I was talking about it being my fault," my mom said, "I didn't just mean encouraging you to get closer to the Corcorans."

"I know," I said.

"I was talking about — the past."

"The past?" I said, trying to play dumb. In the deep, dark recesses of my mind, something stirred, and slowly opened one yellow eye.

"Shannon," my mom said gently but firmly, "when children see their parents in an abusive relationship, it often sets things in place. It can create a pattern."

I was beginning to feel sick to my stomach. "A pattern?"

"Yes." My mom's eyes were locked on mine now, and they were urgent and sad. I didn't want to hear what she was saying, but it seemed like she had to say it to someone. Conundrum. "Sometimes, people wind up being abusers themselves. But other times, they mimic the behaviors they witnessed, and they wind up in abusive relationships, and being abused just as their parents were."

"Is this all stuff you learned in counseling — after?" I said, my voice coming out rougher than I intended. I wasn't feeling very good, and self-protection suddenly seemed very important.

"Don't blow this off, Shan," my mom said, suddenly clutching my arm. Her eyes were wide-open now, and filled with fear. I remembered that look from long ago. "I'd hoped you were too young to remember the worst parts of it, but now I'm afraid. I'm so afraid for you, honey." Her eyes filled again.

I wanted to pull away, but she had a vice grip on my forearm. "Mom, this is going to work out. I broke up with her. It's over."

"Is it?" Her eyes looked almost wild, as though she were seeing horror movies flash across my face. "Do you honestly think I believe you when you tell me this was a *drive-by*? As though it were something *random*?"

I didn't know what to say to that.

"This is the worst time," she went on urgently. "When they've been hurt. We were in hiding, remember? That's when the threats got really bad. That's when the attack at The Excelsior came."

"I remember," I said. The hospital room felt as though it were a python, slowly squeezing me in its coils. It was getting harder and harder to keep my breathing normal.

"That girl could hurt you even worse than she already has," my mom said, starting to cry again. "Shan, what if she'd *killed* you? What if those misfired bullets were meant for you, or you and me?"

"I don't think they were supposed to kill me," I said, slowly realizing something and thinking out loud. "They were meant as a warning. Sonya and Theo were used as… as messages."

"Frankie sent warnings, too," she rejoined, wiping her eyes. "Remember?"

"I spent a long time trying to forget," I said.

"I know," she said. "She was such a sad, angry person."

And my mother looked at me, looked at me in that confused way people do right before they suddenly have a great illumination that changed everything they'd ever thought or assumed up till now. And then, they turn your world upside down, too, and nothing is ever the same afterwards. And my stomach crashes to the basement, like an elevator that's snapped its cables.

Of course I let Kallie abuse me.

My mother's female partner had abused me, too.

Oh God.

Oh God…

I am in the bathroom, vomiting and vomiting and vomiting until I can vomit no more. I slam my head against the tile, trying to black out. From far in the distance, beyond the closed door, I hear my mother call my name. I cover my ears, squeeze my head between my arms, try to trash-compact myself into nothingness. I don't want to exist.

My phone buzzes. I look at it. It's Her.

OMG EDDIE ARRESTED — I THINK HE DID SOMETHING TERRIBLE — PLEASE CALL ME ASAP I NEED YOU-HELP ME PLEASE HELP ME

Chapter 21

I can't remember the last morning I woke up feeling good.

This time, I woke up in the hospital hallway, curled up between two chairs pushed together. It wasn't visiting hours; they must have made an exception for me.

Or maybe I'd said I didn't want to be in my mom's room. Yes. I vaguely remembered that. Me crying, and puke encrusted all over my mouth, and my shirt stained. Me screaming and crying, and the doctor telling me I needed to calm down. My mom crying, holding out her arms to me as I slammed out of her room, down the hallway, trying not to tear my eyes out like Oedipus. I was a raging, sobbing, snuggling, barf-smelling troglodyte. I somehow fell asleep in the waiting area, probably looking like a homeless person; nurses hovering over me.

That's how I felt: homeless. Alone. Bereft. All those years of lying. All that crap.

My phone buzzed: a text from Sonya.

UP YET? SORRY WE DIDN'T SAY GOODBYE LAST NITE U WERE IN THE BATHROOM. SEE U TODAY? HOWS MOM?

How's Mom? I really couldn't care less; I was too upset to talk to her. And I didn't want to deal with Sonya's prying and questions, and Zip—

God! Zip! The person who'd initially confused me when we met was actually one of my greatest champions. So much made sense now, in the cold, gray light of morning.

Frankie's five beers a night. The weekend litany of football games on ESPN. The nights spent at the Horseshoe Bar and Grill, playing Keno and cards in the back, chain smoking while at home my mom cooked me dinner and put me to bed. No friends came over or called. It was a tiny universe of three, built on an illusion of security and control.

Frankie was tough — that's how she saw herself, as if playing a role. Tough, butt-kicking, butch, taking care of a lonely, helpless divorcee and her little boy. Frankie finally had a family, and she was the head of it.

And then one day, the lady and her little boy both got tired of the endless yelling, the throwing things, the broken appliances and dishes, the shoving and the grabbing and the pushing up against walls, and they disappeared. And Frankie snapped.

I didn't even know what prison she went to, I thought. All I knew was that after the trial, Frankie eventually died of lung cancer behind bars. My mom had cried for a day when she heard the news, but then, for the first time in years, she seemed to actually recapture a lightness of spirit, to be free and happy. She'd started her new job, and we'd moved to our new house: not fancy, but home. The Venice jar, still only about half full, sat on my mom's bedroom dresser, but no more change disappeared from it. And we'd somehow cobbled together a life over the past four-plus years, and not looked back.

I didn't cry when I'd heard Frankie had died. Odd, considering as you'd probably figured out, I could be something of a crier. But I'd never shed a tear, even if she'd been the closest thing I'd had to a second parent for three years.

Which was worse: never having something, or having something where the bad outweighed the good? That was kind of the make-or-break question for the weekend.

I suddenly sat bolt upright. *Theo.* That's what I wanted: I wanted to see Theo.

***

I thought Theo was asleep when I poked my head into his hospital room and whispered his name, but he immediately rolled over and grinned at me sleepily, as though he'd been waiting for me. His arm and shoulder were all trussed up with bandages, but I didn't see any blood. "Shan!"

"Not too loud," I hissed, looking over my shoulder. "I'm not sure it's visiting hours yet."

"What happened to *you*?" Theo said, his eyes wide. I'd momentarily forgotten how disheveled I must've looked, and how much I probably smelled.

"Long night," I said, deciding not to get into it for now. "Worried about my mom. She's fine now," I added hurriedly, lest he start asking questions. "Just stress from everything."

"*Yeah,*" Theo drawled. "A little stressful, that's a good way to put it. I thought my parents were going to snap like twigs. But the operation was a success."

"It was?" Finally, some good news.

"Yeah," he grinned, flooding the room with his own brand of sunshine. "The bullet grazed my arm pretty badly, but it totally missed the bone. It's probably lodged in Sonya's upstairs hallway," he added, still grinning. "Hope they find it: I'd love to wear it as a necklace."

"You're a nut-job," I said, sitting on the edge of the bed and finally feeling my body relax, and a smile come over my face.

"You know it. Surviving getting shot will do that to you," Theo quipped. "The bad news is, I can't swim for a few weeks while things are healing. The good news is, they don't anticipate permanent damage. It's only the first week, I've got time to train myself back up to speed."

"You're gonna need some extra-special workouts," I said.

"You volunteering to help with them?" he returned with another grin. Then the grin wavered a bit, maybe as he remembered the front seat of his car barely twenty-four hours prior.

"I might," I said carefully. "If you'd let me."

"I'd let you," he said. "Workouts, that is."

I nodded, and there was a long pause where we didn't seem to know what to say, so we kind of looked away, then looked back at each other, then looked away again. Eventually, Theo put up his hand for a shake. I did it carefully, and he scooched forward and draped himself against me for a moment.

"I'm so sorry," I said into the shoulder of his hospital gown.

"Me too." He finally did that double back-slap thing guys do when they're trying to tell you it's time to stop hugging, and pulled back to rest on his pillows again. "But at least it's all over."

"What is?"

"The Corcorans," Theo said. "Didn't you hear? It was all over late-night TV news last night. I was dozing in and out, but I got most of it. Eddie's been arrested."

"I heard," I said, holding up my phone so he could read Kallie's text.

He did. His face noticeably darkened. "Shan—"

"I have to see her one more time," I said, articulating it out loud for the first time.

"Are you *crazy?*" Theo almost yelled the last word. I winced. A nurse poked her head in and looked at us, then disappeared, presumably in search of a doctor.

Theo was looking at me as though I'd announced I was jumping off the Empire State building. "Shan, *why?*"

"We didn't really talk yesterday," I said slowly, trying to organize my thoughts. "I have things I need to say to her. And she's done, she has no power over me any more, now that I've figured out some stuff." (I decided not to go into detail as to what the 'stuff' was.) "And she's a wreck, with Eddie being arrested. The least I can do is take the high road."

"She could hurt you again," Theo said, darkly.

"She won't," I said. "Haven't you figured it out? She might have wanted to hurt Sonya and Zip, but she can't now. It's Eddie who was responsible for yesterday." I gave him a significant look. "Probably because of you."

"Me?" Theo looked genuinely thrown.

"Didn't you notice how he was looking at you yesterday?" I asked, letting my voice fill with portent.

"I was a little scattered yesterday," Theo said, a slight edge creeping into his voice. "Mostly due to helping you with *your* issues."

"Gee, thanks," I said, nettled.

"Oh come *on*, Shan!" Theo almost roared; good thing he didn't currently have a hospital roommate. "Can't you see she's playing you again? She cries, and you go scurrying off like her little bitch!"

"She's never cried," I said, carefully. I liked Theo: I didn't want to lose someone else close to me. "And I'm not her bitch; at least, not any more. She wrote on the mirror FACE YOUR FEAR, remember? If I just let this ride, I *will* still always be her bitch."

"She still has pictures of you," Theo muttered, almost sulkily.

"And I can watch her delete them."

The sunshine was gone. Theo looked like a storm cloud coming over the ridge. Without thinking, I went to the worst place I could've gone: "Look, you don't have to be all jealous…"

"*Jealous?*" Theo stared at me, incredulous. "Of what? Of *her?*"

"Maybe you resent that your ex-boyfriend's in jail now," I said, sounding snottier than I'd meant to. "Maybe you're just pissed at me, because I wasn't the one who got barred from the Corcoran's in the first place. Maybe," I shot back, flushing crimson, "you're just messed up because you want me, but you're afraid to act on it!"

"Get out," Theo said, all warmth and friendliness drained from his face. "Get out of here, Shannon. Go do whatever the hell you want. Go kiss up to her; go be a white knight, whatever." He looked at me with a mixture of pity, contempt, and something close to hatred. "Hell, go screw her one more time, if that's what you're hoping for! Will that make you feel like a *real* man? Maybe she'll finally let you be on top!"

I jumped off the bed so quickly it shifted, and I landed right beside him. Without thinking about it, as if it were a natural reflex, my right hand came around and glanced off the side of his face. It still made a *smacking* sound. Half an inch over, it would've been a full-on slap.

That was the moment Sonya and Zip walked in.

There was an audible gasp from Sonya, and Zip fell back against the wall. Theo's face collapsed into an angry red morass, the sobs sounding like they were exploding out of him.

I whirled, almost collided with Zip, who looked like he'd been the one who'd been struck, and made contact with Sonya, whose face still showed a webbing of scratches. She looked at me as though I were the Tasmanian devil from those old cartoons, a whirling dervish of out-of-control emotions.

"I'm sorry," I choked to Theo, to everyone. "I'm sorry, I'm sorry, I'm *sorry!*"

I slammed my fist against a wall, just as Frankie might have during a fit, and ran out the door and down the hallway. Behind me, I could hear Theo's cries and blubbering, as Zip and Sonya moved to him. I ran past my mom's room, as she called out "Shannon!" with a voice that sounded like someone at the bottom of a well, but I didn't stop.

I ran down the hallway past the waiting area, the nurses' station, the flock of fluttering women all calling out to me: "Slow down!" "What's wrong?" "Where are you going?" A chorus of voices yelling at me, around me, inside me. Voices I tried to outrun. Voices I couldn't outrun.

I ran, and ran, and ran.

I ran out of the hospital and ran all the way back to school, where my mom's car was waiting. I drove home, the road barely visible through my tears. I ran in the house, turned on the shower as hot as I could stand it, ripped off my clothes, and dove under the cascade of steaming water. I stayed there as long as I could, until my breathing returned to normal, until I felt like I had burned every last rotten and sinful thing out of myself.

Now, I moved in slow motion, as though I were Pinocchio underwater, dragging a rock behind his donkey tail, picking out my nicest dress shirt, my best slacks, a tie. I carefully combed my hair, brushed my teeth. I scrutinized my reddened, little-boy face. I looked like a choirboy ready for his first Communion, or someone about to face execution.

Then, I picked up my phone and texted her.

I'M ON MY WAY.

Chapter 22

Driving up to the Corcoran's in a car, even if it was my mom's ancient Jetta, still made me feel more empowered than the previous time when I biked up here in a sweaty mess, or when I rode like royalty in the passenger seat of Kallie's BMW. I was listening to some sort of thrash metal on the stereo — Slipknot, or who knew what — something to get my aggression up. I wanted to walk into that house with my balls clanking, and show her who was boss once and for all.

The driveway was empty, but I was expecting that.

This time, however, no one came to open my car door, nor even the front door. Where was Parsons? A flood of shame came over me: I was actually expecting to be waited on. Me, whose mom had always tried to teach the value of hard work, and to never take anything for granted. Man, the past week really messed me up, I thought grimly.

My phone chirped. Was she watching from inside?

DOWN AT THE POOL HOUSE—MOM & DAD TALKING TO LAWYER, PARSONS HAS DAY OFF. COME ON IN/DOWN, WAITING FOR YOU.

Rather than walk around the entire perimeter of the house, I decided to cut through. I tried the front door: it was unlocked.

I stepped in, feeling a strange sense of dishevelment in the air. On my previous visits, everything in this house had felt in place and meticulously put together. Now, there was an indefinable sense of something askew. Yet everything looked the same: same beautifully laid, dining-room table, same giant screen TV, same fancy weaponry attached to the walls. But there were no people; no smell of food cooking, no music, no magazines or books open mid-read. The place seemed like the world's fanciest vacation rental.

I moved through the kitchen to the door and looked down at the pool. Kallie was down there on the same chaise I saw her sitting on the other day, but this time she was in a little hunched ball, wearing an oversized T-shirt to seemingly protect herself against the coolness of the morning. Even from this distance, she looked so vulnerable and sad, I could feel a wave of sympathy and kindness towards her starting to wash over me, until I remembered the night at the Excelsior, and the pictures, and the swim meet yesterday. *"Face your fear"* indeed. Bitch, you have no idea what was about to come at you.

I walked down the path to the pool, scanning the sky. It was only mid-sixties now, but you could feel it was going to get a lot warmer later in the day. Everything seemed ultra-vivid: the little flowers in the landscaping popped out against the brown of the dirt, the stone patio sparkled in the morning sun, and the water was a dazzling aquamarine. I could hear my shoes going *clack-clack-clack* as I strode purposefully down, down.

The sun's reflections from the water were rippling across her face as I walked up and stood before her, looking down on her from on high, my face perfectly composed. "Hi."

"Hi," she said, fidgeting. She didn't look like she'd showered or done much to her hair. She looked up at me, and her face was as guileless and innocent as I'd ever seen it. "Thanks for coming," she said, softly.

"Okay," I said, lowering myself onto one of the other lounge chairs, spreading my legs apart and clasping my hands between them, as though I were awaiting her cues.

There was a long pause where she didn't say anything, just stared at the water lapping against the cement. Far away, a crow cawed; otherwise, it was very quiet.

"There's some lemonade," she murmured, gesturing to the little table where a pale-yellow pitcher stood sweating next to an empty glass. She had a half-full glass in her lap, and one finger distractedly ran around and around the rim.

I poured some and took a big swig, realizing, yet again, I'd come here on an empty stomach. "Thanks," I said.

There was another long pause.

"He started molesting me when I was eight," Kallie said, completely without warning or preface. "Eight. Can you imagine? It went on for almost six years."

I was so startled, I almost dropped the glass I was tipping to my lips. Her eyes shifted suddenly towards me, a statue's face suddenly becoming alive.

"Who?" I said. "Eddie?"

She laughed somewhat bitterly. "*Eddie?* No. Eddie is gay as the day is long. He hasn't been near a pussy since he came out of my mother's." She surveyed the pool, her lip curled in disgust and hatred as she seemed to envision this. "No — my uncle."

That was the missing puzzle piece.

"He used to tuck me into bed," she said, stringing each word as if it were a bead on a rosary; click, click, click. "That's when it would happen. My mother was always cleaning up after dinner, and my father would be watching the sports report. It didn't take long. It got to the point where we could get it done in less than ten minutes. Less chance of discovery for him; over quicker for me." She laughed bitterly. "Eddie used to complain to my parents. 'Why does she get tucked in, and I don't?' Oh, he'd just *wish* our uncle would tuck him in like that."

"Did anyone ever find out?" I asked, afraid of interrupting her. "Does anyone know?"

"No one knows," she went on, her voice sounding like it had been dipped in acid. "All these years, I've never told anyone. You, I thought I could trust. You were kind. Gentle. Maybe you'd be the one who'd help me forget."

She turned her head and looked at me, a long, hard look, as though I were just coming into focus. "But you were *too* nice. Too soft. Too squishy. Too easily misled by others. I kept pushing the envelope with you, wondering how far you'd let me take it." Her mouth twisted. "Pretty damn far, apparently."

"Kallie—" I started to say. All of the high ground I'd been perched on, not five minutes ago, was rapidly crumbling to sand. I was on the defensive again. Again.

"But Theo," she went on musingly. "That was one I didn't see coming. Of course, I didn't think you were queer. Maybe you aren't. Maybe you're bi." She cocked her head, studying me as though I were a specimen in a lab. "But you definitely have some feelings for him, and I think they're reciprocated."

"They're not," I said, a little too defensively. My voice came out a scratchy whisper.

"Oh, you didn't see the way he was looking at you yesterday," she said, her voice sounding like a knife being sharpened. (My God, hadn't I just said something like that to Theo?) "All of them — Sonya, Theo, that he-she thing. Shannon Milne — the *nice* boy." She said the word *nice* as though it turned her stomach.

"I'm not that nice," I said. The sun seemed to be getting warmer. I drained the glass.

"Oh please," she almost snarled. "I was nice once, too. You think I was *always* like this? You think I woke up one day and just said, 'Gee, life's been a tad dull, I think I'll become a living bitch for the *hell* of it?'"

Her eyes flashed, and I had a sickening feeling of history repeating itself.

She sat up and leaned towards me, her sour breath in my face. "Let me tell you: having a relative have sex with you, against your will, *over* and *over* and *over* for *years* will kind of strip away a lot of your *nice* qualities."

"But—" I stammered. All of my tough resolve was gone. I could barely form coherent sentences. "But your friends, your family—"

"My friends are useless. My family runs on appearances and illusions," Kallie said flatly. "Look around. We have parties. My father has business associates to dinner. We *play* family. We pretend we're normal and happy, that everything is fine. It's what happens behind closed doors that's so messed up." She frowned. "Of course, it doesn't help when people like you and Theo don't play ball with us like you're *supposed* to."

"Eddie," I said. "Eddie and you…"

"Oh, Eddie will be fine," she said, almost flippantly. "I wasn't thrilled when he said he wanted to come to the meet with me, but it worked out well. It created a perfect motivation for what happened at Sonya's."

The world felt like it was slowly beginning to tilt on its side. "He shot up Sonya's," I said, speaking what

I thought was a statement but suddenly gleaning a sickening question deep inside of it.

Kallie smiled slowly; the kind of smile that uncoiled itself, like a snake. "Yes, he did. But I made sure he was, shall we say, in an *altered* state of mind before we drove there. After seeing Theo and you, of course he wanted a drink — or two, or three, or six. And I was the one who helped him aim and fire the gun. Wearing gloves, of course." The smile was full-on now. "And then we drove home. The cops came looking for the guy in the driver's seat with the gun in his jacket; not a girl in the passenger seat who'd been helping him steer. And he was too messed up at that point to offer up any sort of coherent defense."

"Why?

"Why do you *think*?!" she shouted. The Kallie I knew from all last week was now fully awake and engaged. "There were — are — *too many people* between us. I just want to… thin them out."

"You can't *thin out* people," I said groggily. Jesus, the sun was melting me like butter on an iron skillet. I was sweating profusely, and just forming words seemed to take a tremendous amount of effort.

"Yes, I can," she said. "It'll be all over the news tonight. How your so-called friends came up here, looking for you, and overpowered me: me here, all by myself, so alone and helpless." She fluttered her eyes at me, the picture of vulnerability. "How I *had* to defend myself, and how sad it is that I had to shoot them in self-defense, before they killed me."

"They won't come," I said, wiping my brow and trying to stay upright. Something was wrong. Something was wrong, something was very, very wrong with me.

"They'll come," she said confidently. "They'll come because I'll use your phone to send a message to get them up here."

"We had a fight…" I said, woozy beyond words. "I said… awful things."

"You underestimate yourself," she said. "They'll come. And I'll be waiting."

"I'll never give you my phone," I said, trying to stand, reaching into my pocket for it in the hope that I could throw it in the pool, but I immediately fell back on the chaise lounge. The world, now scalding hot, was beginning to spin. I didn't know if I was going to suffocate, incinerate, or just fall off the edge.

"Yeah you will," she said, tapping the lemonade pitcher as she looked down at me. "Oh yeah, you will."

She never drank anything, I suddenly realized through the haze. She'd been holding her glass the whole time, but I'd never seen her put it to her lips. Clever, clever girl. God only knew what that lemonade had been spiked with.

"Good night, Sleeping Beauty," Kallie said, reaching over my prone body as the world began to darken and fade. She brushed a finger down the side of my face and kissed my cheek, letting her lips linger against it. There was nothing tender about the gesture. *You're my bitch,* the kiss said.

It took everything I had, before I sank into nothingness, to summon up a wad of phlegm from the lemonade and spit at her. Then came the *slap,* and my neck snapped to the side, and everything went purple and then, finally, black.

And in the darkness, I felt the handcuffs click into place around my wrists again.

Chapter 23

I am jerked awake by a sound. My head throbs, and my gut feels nauseous yet again. I roll over and puke the remainder of whatever is left in my stomach, which, after the past couple days, isn't much.

I am lying on the concrete next to the pool; one hand is still handcuffed to the stair railing. The sun is medium-low in the sky and scalding. Everything is hyper-illuminated in an orange and red glow. It must be the afternoon, late afternoon.

I try to pull myself up, but my wrist pulls against the steel, and I feel it crushing against the bone. I heard something that woke me up; something that caused me to flinch and flail.

A gunshot.

Then another. Then another.

I am having another full-on panic attack. I want to move, but can't. I try to scream, but can barely open my cracked lips to emit a croaking groan. I don't know what's happening, and I'm terrified to find out.

Then all hell breaks loose.

Kallie, crouching in and around the bushes, runs down the stairs, dives into the bushes, lies almost flat, fires a shot up the hill. From the house, I hear return fire. One shot in return.

Jesus God, what is going on?

Kallie scrabbles her way down the hill, fires another shot. There's return fire from above again. One of the bullets whizzes above the pool, but another hits the cement not twenty feet away from me.

Whoever is up there, they'd better know how to aim.

"Drop it!" Kallie calls, her voice pure steel. "Shan's down here. You're going to hit him!"

"He'd better be alive," returns a female voice, coolly.

Sonya!

"He is," Kallie calls, backing carefully around the edge of the pool towards me, gun raised and pointed up the hillside. "But if you keep firing at me, you'll turn him into Swiss cheese!"

"Just don't hurt him," Sonya calls back, imperiously. She sounds seriously badass.

Kallie is behind me, gun still in her hand. Her cheeks are pink and glowing, and a manic glitter is in her green, green eyes. She presses the gun to my head with her left hand while her right hand unlocks the handcuffs. "Don't do anything stupid," she says in a low growl. "Somehow they got the gun safe open, and they're armed. That wasn't part of the plan."

"No, the plan was you were going to lead them like lambs to slaughter," I groan. "They weren't supposed to fight back." I wonder if Theo knew the combination. He would if Eddie told it to him.

She hits me with the butt of the gun. "Shut up," she growls. I am momentarily stunned. She pulls my hands together and refastens the cuffs around them, so now I am free of the railing, but cuffed from behind. "What do you think? Shall we go for a little boat ride?" She rolls me into the water and pushes me forward, as if I were a float.

I try to struggle, but I'm still too dizzy, sick, and disoriented, and now, apparently, bleeding from the head, as I watch a vapor of red flow past my eyes into the pale blue depths. I roll over and try to keep my face and head above water. Kallie punches me in the stomach and I buckle, doubling up, swallowing a whole mouthful of pool water.

So this is what it's like wrestling with a sea monster.

So this is what it's like knowing you're about to die.

She pulls me up, spluttering and coughing, by the hair; she lets me feel the gun against my temple again. Her voice is cool, but tense. "Nice try, sweetie."

"Kallie — you need to let him go."

I somehow flop-turn myself at an angle, and stare across the pool at Sonya. She is wearing a black T-shirt and jeans and looks fifty feet tall, and is walking slowly towards the edge of the pool, one gun tucked in the waistband of her skirt, and a shotgun held in front of her, both hands aiming it firmly at Kallie and me. She looks like an avenging goddess-warrior from a comic book. I have never been so glad to see someone in my life.

"I *need*?" Kallie's voice is harsh. "Oh, you don't get to tell me what I need."

"There's no good ending here," Sonya says, trying to sound reasonable, but a note of cool contempt is in her voice. "My father took me deer and duck hunting for years. You might hit me, eventually. I *will* hit you."

"Not if you hit Shan, too," Kallie says, positioning my body right in front of her and crouching in the pool. My clothes, sopping wet, cling to me like so much debris, further restricting my movements; as if the gun at my head wasn't already a powerful incentive not to move.

"Kallie," Sonya says, trying to sound reasonable. "This is endgame. We know what you tried to do. Shan knows it. You seriously think you can get out of this with no consequences? You're looking at prison time, even without killing one of us."

"Maybe I'll just kill all of you, and then myself," Kallie says bitterly. "You think I have anything to live for after this? All I ever wanted was for someone to love me. Really love me."

"You sure got a screwed-up way of showing it," I say bitterly, against my better judgment. Kallie pistol-whips me again; my whole body feels the pain.

I'm sorry, Mom. I'm sorry, everybody. I'm so, so, sorry…

Sonya cocks the shotgun. I can hear the click-click from all the way over where I am. "Do that again, Kallie, and I'll take the shot."

"Go ahead!" Kallie yells, rage as always finally getting the better of her. "You think I'm afraid of you? You think any of you are so smart? Go ahead—"

Ca-chick!

That's not a gunshot! I have about .03 of a second to think.

A scream rips through the air, and Kallie's body jerks away from me. In her upper chest, right next to where she was holding the pistol to my head, is a scary-looking arrow.

Ca-chick!

Then another one whizzes us past us into the water.

I am flailing and splashing and trying to stay afloat. I flop over in the water just long enough to see Zip emerge from the bushes on the other side of the pool, a crossbow from the living room display still in his hands.

"Shan! Get away from her!"

I somehow throw my body forward, but with my shoes and clothes on, it's an effort. The air is ripped apart by two gunshots — one from behind me, and one from in front of me.

I can't get loose, can't turn over. I open my mouth to call for help, and swallow a couple lungsful of water. Everything I've ever known about swimming till this point is useless when you're dressed, handcuffed, bleeding from a head wound, and still waking up from some sort of sleeping-pill cocktail.

I see the surface of the water and the sky drifting further and further away, and in the corner of the pool, far above me, Kallie's silhouette floating on her back, bleeding rivulets of blood from her chest and shoulder.

I'm beginning to black out again… oh God…

"Shan! Get Shan!"

A SPLASH of water. Two bodies throw themselves in, next to me, grab me, pull me up to the surface. Gasping and choking and trying to get my lungs to work, I clutch at my saviors, panic finally convulsing me. We move slowly to the shallow end, inch by inch, foot by foot, as I am dimly aware of Sonya looming over Kallie, reaching down to remove the pistol from her hand, cell phone at her ear. "Yes, 911…"

And then two sets of arms are cradling me, touching my face, gently slapping me awake. "Is he okay?" "Think his lungs are full." "Let's get him over here and lay him down."

Zip. And Theo, still bandaged, still not fully functional in one arm, but there. Kallie was right and I was wrong: even after everything, they came.

They hold me close between them, keep me safe, let the water and nasty gunk run out of my nose and mouth and lungs as I cough, and gag, and in general am pretty gross and disgusting and repellent, because that's what friends do.

There is the sound of sirens again, of running steps. Cops and paramedics are pouring down the stairs to us. I listen to the raspy breathing of my lungs, clutch Zip's hand, feel Theo stroking my hair as the sun sets. "Hey, bud," he whispers.

I look over at Kallie as she floats, stares at us, no expression on her face, her eyes wide with incomprehension as my friends care for me. Somehow, I am able to summon just enough strength to whisper to her.

"This is what it's like when someone loves you."

Her eyes might have narrowed; I'm not sure. Then many hands are on us, around us, and we're all being pulled out of the pool.

I do not see her again.

Chapter 24

I'm sitting in Catch, on a jazz-combo night. I've got my best dress shirt — deep blue — and black slacks on. I'm even wearing a tie.

The music is swinging, and people are having a great time. I sneak another look at my mom, working the lobby, so elegant and refined in her long purple dress, silver earrings dangling against her skin. She sees me looking, and smiles at me.

I feel hyper-attuned to everything tonight. The candles seem to glow warmer than they ever have, the music is right in the groove, and I'm looking forward to a big bowl of chowder to warm my insides.

But I see the man sitting by himself again; the man who used to come in here with his wife. Then they started coming less and less frequently, and when they did she would wear a stylish headscarf turban-style, to cover up the results of the chemotherapy. Then they stopped coming altogether.

My last memory of them was a night in October, when I'd just set another school record and had come here with Theo, Sonya, and Zip to celebrate. He'd worn a vintage white dinner jacket, and she'd worn a sort of Middle Eastern-style dress in peacock blue and green, with a jewel at the front of the turban. The way he'd gently taken his wife's frail arm to help her rise from her chair, and draped her jacket around her shoulders as he ushered them out of the restaurant, caught my attention.

"What'cha looking at?" Zip asked, smiling at me. He'd worn a coat and tie that night, and had freshly-cut his hair, so he looked exceptionally handsome.

"Nothing. An old couple I like to watch."

Sonya lifted an eyebrow, an elegant smirk moving across her lips. She wore a silver gown with long earrings, and she looked like a supermodel. Next to her, in an emerald-green dress shirt, that showed off his shaggy blond hair, was Theo. He smiled at me, too.

"You're just a soft heart, Shan," Theo said.

"Nothing wrong with that," Sonya returned, buttering a roll with flourish as if she were a Duchess at the palace. "That's why we love him."

"Guys," I said, embarrassed.

"Oh!" Zip squealed. "It's *The Wizard of Oz*! Shannon is the Tin Man, Sonya is Dorothy, and with those shaggy curls Theo can be the Lion…"

"You realize that you just made yourself the Scarecrow with no brain," Theo said with a grin.

"Oh yeah," Zip deflated. "Maybe I can be the Horse of a Different Color? Or a flying monkey!"

"And I'll be the tree that throws apples," Sonya shot back.

"I sense a group Halloween costume," I laughed. What a concept. I'd spent most of my life feeling like I was always in costume every day, as a normal kid; now, I'd actually get to dress up for fun with friends.

"To us," Zip said, holding up a glass of Diet Coke.

"*L'chaim*, darling," Sonya said, clinking his glass with her lemonade.

"What's that mean?" Theo asked, clinking his soda glass anyways.

"To life," I said. "It's a sweet ride."

"If you have the right company," Sonya said, winking at me.

They were funny. They were kind. They were mine. How lucky was I?

And now, the old man catches my eye again. He watches the musicians, and I can see tears glittering in his eyes. The chair next to him is empty. He clutches a napkin in his fist, twists it around and around, as if he needs something to cling onto; something that will keep him afloat.

I whisper to Sheila, and leave my little booth, make my way through the crowd by zig-zagging around the tables. I dodge waiters with trays of steaming hot food, nod to the bass player, who recognizes me now, and move around past the little stage, and I'm standing in front of the old man.

He looks up at me, momentarily confused, and I again notice the piece of cloth in his hands. It's not a napkin. It looks like a handkerchief; a very elegant old-school handkerchief. The kind his wife would've used.

He's picking at a seafood salad, but it looks like he doesn't have much of an appetite. The chair next to him is still empty.

"Hi," I say. "I'm Shan Milne. Fiona's son."

"Oh — yes," the man says, his eyes flicking to the lobby. "Fiona. Of course. You look just like her."

"Thank you," I say, not blushing. I appreciate the compliment.

"She's always been so kind to me and— my wife," the man says. Tears are shining in his eyes again. "She'd always give us the best seats and the nicest servers. I mean, when I used to bring my wife here…" He leaves the sentence and the thought hanging in the air.

I take a breath. "May I join you for dinner?" I ask. It's still hard for me to be so direct and forthright sometimes. But the old man's smile lights up the whole room.

"I'd like that very much," he says. As I slide into the booth, he says, "So, I hear you're quite the swimmer."

"I can be," I say.

Chapter 25

It's a rainy Sunday afternoon in November. Christmas is coming soon, the radio is already starting to sneak the occasional carol onto the playlist.

We've been busy for the last couple hours, and now we're lying in my bed, warm and cozy and snuggled up together under the soft, flannel sheets. Rain is on the window, the desk-light providing the only illumination. My mom won't be home till late tonight, so we have time for dinner, and maybe another go-round later.

I'm still amazed at the wonder of a naked body, of skin under my fingertips. To have someone close to you, breathing with you, exhaling in your ear, murmuring your name over and over. To taste the sweetness of sweat. To be together as one being. To know what it is to be loved, to give love, to make love.

To love someone more than yourself.

To feel desired.

To feel treasured.

To feel safe.

To feel like you're the best person you can be.

And you'd probably like to know: who am I with? Sonya, Zip or Theo?

And my answer is: does it matter?

I'm Shan Milne.
And I'm happy.